Pretty White Lies

Pretty White Lies

MARY CANTELL

RESOURCE *Publications* · Eugene, Oregon

PRETTY WHITE LIES

Resource Publications
An Imprint of Wipf and Stock Publishers
199 W. 8th Ave., Suite 3
Eugene, OR 97401

www.wipfandstock.com

PAPERBACK ISBN: 979-8-3852-5820-8
HARDCOVER ISBN: 979-8-3852-5821-5
EBOOK ISBN: 979-8-3852-5822-2

VERSION NUMBER 11/03/25

To my beloved husband, my love,
and to the memory of my precious mother,
who fostered the writing bud in me
to bloom, my thanks, always . . .

The heart is deceitful above all things and desperately wicked . . . who can know it?

—JEREMIAH 17:9

Acknowledgments

Officer Juan Mercado #9431, Philadelphia Police Marine Unit

Corporal Kyle Reeser, Gettysburg State Police

Plymouth Township Police Department personnel

Trayce Duran, senior editor

Prologue

Just before dusk, Marly's nerves tensed as she drove through the park. The drive home often relaxed her as the scenic beauty of the rolling landscape soothed her daily stressors. Tonight felt different. There was nothing particularly unusual at this hour except the car in the rearview mirror had been there a while. Was the driver tailing her or just in a hurry? Of course, her overactive imagination could be lending to her paranoia. While life wasn't always a scary movie, her untethered thoughts could easily make it one. Logically, there was no need to cast unnecessary suspicion. Being a Type A personality, and with so much on her plate while juggling multiple tasks, she often made up lost time while on the road. Maybe the driver was Type A, too. She glanced in the mirror again and tapped the brakes, hoping the person would get the hint and back off a bit.

On a typical drive home through the park, people were often on the foot paths walking their dogs in the early evening. A horse and rider occasionally meandered alongside the road. Oddly, there was no one around. Even the parking area was empty. As she maneuvered the curving twists and turns of the road, the car traveling behind was still there; its presence glared as though with a vendetta. She breathed in a calming breath, but the calm didn't come. Unless it was her imagination again, the car seemed to be even closer. When she sped up to put distance between them, the driver mirrored her speed. It would be impossible to go any faster, especially with the narrowness of the road. She gripped the wheel tighter. Her palms grew damp. A bad feeling stirred in her stomach.

Chapter One

I NEED TO SEE *you in my office.*

His words took Marly by surprise. The nine syllables no employee ever wants to hear from a boss. Even the simple phrase, *we need to talk,* could be daunting. Had she done something wrong?

John Strauss, VP of Operations at MNN, always appeared to be troubled. The perpetual vertical lines etched between his brows were his signature statement. The key was to figure out whether it was his own personal issue or something else that caused his edgy demeanor. Judging from his current vibe, Marly couldn't tell, but the sound of his voice carried the onerous clang of a death knell. Though the toll of actual death would ring softer than intimidating words because death didn't sting or sear; it lent that kind of misfortune only to the living.

In the fast-paced environment of a multi-media news network in Philadelphia where Marly worked, the players struggled to retain their coveted on-air positions. Competition remained fierce in this cut-throat business. It was all anyone could do to keep one's head above water, above the fray, and know whose butt to kiss every now and then. Like a 3-D chess match, the players were always in motion. Though Marly never quite knew how to play the game, she was smart enough to keep herself out of office politics. Her only angle was to work hard.

As soft as the leather chair was in John Strauss's office, it may as well have been the electric chair for all the comfort it lent. Marly never felt at ease sitting there, though maybe this time she'd be getting a good word from him. She held high hopes and had nothing to regret.

In the chill of his overly cool office, Marly tucked both hands underneath her legs while waiting for her boss to get off the phone. Her mind flashed back to her first day here at the network doing live TV reporting on a frigidly cold day—the time Philadelphia had been hit with a powerful nor'easter.

"Ten seconds, Marly," the cameraman shouted over the gust of wind that blew her hair. Aware that thousands would soon be focusing on her image, her stomach danced. She remembered a colleague's words about being nervous while on camera. "Just pretend you're talking to a friend. You've got this, girl."

She loved her job. Though live on-air broadcasting lent less fear than sitting now in John Strauss's office.

Her boss hung up the phone. He placed his elbows on the desktop and steepled his fingers. "Marly,"—he blew out a breath—"listen, I'm sorry, Marly, to have to tell you this, but I have some bad news." Her stomach cinched tighter. "With the budget cuts, and I'm sure you're aware that we need to cut corners . . . please understand that it's not personal, but I'm afraid we're taking you off your assignment." His next words landed like a bomb. "The worst of it is, we have to let you go."

Her heart sunk. *Not personal?*

Deep down, Marly knew there had to be some reason she was singled out for a layoff. What about the others who'd been hired after her? Were those necks on the chopping block, too? Did Christine Kirsh make the cut? She'd only been there a year or so after her internship. Still a novice in Marly's opinion. While he didn't offer any consolation that she was in the same boat as others, she wondered who would be taking up the story she so diligently pursued? Marly knew she had the goods to deliver on her job and had already invested time and effort into one of the hottest cases on the Main Line. This was *her* project. Would anyone else be able to tackle it with as much determination or conviction? *How could this be happening?*

"What about the story?" Her voice sounded wounded in her ears.

"What story is that?" John steepled his fingers.

Did he not know? "My story . . . the one I've been working on," she shot back, her voice rising. "The death of the little girl on the Main Line, Libby Kirshka."

John Strauss's face reddened in the light of his desk lamp. "Oh . . . ah, well, I-I went to bat for you, Marly. I really tried to get them to . . . uh . . . " he rambled on, stuttering as he went.

Her brain no longer registered the rest of what he had to say; his words became a blur. Investigative news was everything she'd aspired to. Despite her wrenched heart in light of being let go, it was no worse than the injustice of letting the story rot on the vine. No, there would be justice for the child. This was *not* the end.

Most perplexing was the way her boss's face reddened when explaining the situation. He couldn't look her in the eye and began to stutter. John Strauss never stuttered in all the years she'd known him. He was bold and persuasive, never retreating or looking away. Something didn't sit well.

Chapter Two

MARLY EYED THE BOTTLE of sangria. The dark red wine sparkled in the candlelight. Fruity enough to quench her taste as well as assuage her mood. She reached for the bottle and poured a glass.

Her husband frowned. "Easy, honey, you know wine hits you hard."

"It's only my second glass, Craig." *Or third?* She raised the rim to her lips. "Besides, I just lost my job. Gotta celebrate somehow." Marly savored the wine, hoping it would lift her spirits. *Spirits for spirits. It should work that way.* Why else do people imbibe or become alcoholics? Though she hoped to never cross that line.

Marly cast a glance around the room. The old farmhouse restaurant still maintained its charming ambiance—fresh-cut flowers, murals of the French countryside, rustic wood beams. Nothing much changed since the time she and Craig held their wedding reception here, the time her happiness was at a pinnacle. Who wouldn't be happy to be getting married to him? Craig was handsome, successful, and the love of her life. Whenever he gave her a wink, it made her heart melt. If only her life could have kept up so well. She still loved Craig and their marriage was secure, at least as far as she could tell. Though there was that *one* time he disappeared on her on a Saturday afternoon without notice or even a call. But that was a long time ago.

"You look like you're somewhere else," he said.

"I was just thinking about the last time we were here. Remember Dee's toast to us? *To the greatest couple I know, congratulations.* And then she spilled her wine."

He nodded with a grin.

"Seven years . . . I can't believe it's been seven years already, and that poor girl still isn't married." She raised the glass to her lips. "What's wrong with Ethan, anyway?"

"Ethan? You're blaming Ethan?"

"Don't you think it's odd that Dee and Ethan aren't married yet? C'mon, it's been like over a decade they've been dating."

"You're saying it's Ethan's fault?"

"It's always the guy." She waved her hand, dismissively.

"How's that? He's apparently not the marrying kind is all."

"What does that even mean? So, Dee's not good enough for him?"

"What can I say? Some guys just wanna be bachelors."

"Oh, that's crap. He already tied the knot once before, Craig. Besides, after dating like forever, he doesn't know what he'd be getting? And she cleans his house every week like a wife would so—"

"Or a maid," he interjected.

"True. He *does* pay her to do it. So, what's the difference?"

"Maybe he just doesn't want to risk it again."

"Risk what?"

"Maybe she's not Ms. Right. Ever think of that? Maybe they're just a tired habit at this point . . . not happy but living settled."

"I felt bad when I first showed her my engagement ring. I could tell it was bittersweet for her. Once again, she would be the bridesmaid and not the bride."

Marly took another sip of wine as she recalled the strapping Ethan lean over to pat Craig on the shoulder, extending his hand. "Best of luck, man," he'd said to Craig, and as the two pals since forever stood facing each other shaking hands, a broad grin spread on Craig's face.

"You're next, guy."

Ethan rolled his eyes. "Not sure about that, buddy." He blushed and then winked at her before leaving with Dee.

Marly gulped the last of her wine amid her reverie and reached once again for the bottle sitting by Craig's elbow. Craig gently pulled it away from her grasp.

"Cra-ig!"

"Nice try, girl. I think we've had enough for one night. You've had three glasses and you're 105 pounds." A smirk twitched on his lips. "Want me to have to carry you out of here?"

Marly heaved an exaggerated sigh and picked at the remains of cheesecake with her fork. Soon the waitress came back and placed the bill on the table along with two tiny chocolate mints wrapped in green foil.

"Something else bothering you?"

Marly shook her head.

"Yes, there is."

Silence.

"You gonna tell me?"

"That little girl."

"Still?" He put his elbows on the table, cupping his hands.

"I'm not giving up on her." Marly dropped her fork decidedly on the plate. "I may not be getting paid to investigate anymore, but that story still haunts me."

"Marly, it's cold. It'll be tough." His face tensed with concern.

"I know. I'm just obsessed. I'm fascinated that no one has discovered anything more about her. It's unnerving to me. It's like the JonBenét Ramsey case. Only this one is going to get solved."

"Is it really worth it?"

"Why do you say that?"

He shrugged.

"If it were your child, wouldn't you want to find out the truth? I can't be the only one haunted by it."

"I'm sure you're not, hon,"—he pulled out his credit card and placed it in the leather folder—"but all I know is that curiosity killed the cat."

Chapter Three

THE FAMILIAR SCENT OF paper and ink permeated the air, along with the aroma of polished wood. The remembrance of long-ago days washed over Marly in a nostalgic rush. She hadn't set foot inside a library in ages; the memories had all been good and now came back to her as she meandered through the book stacks admiring the dedication of writers throughout the ages. She loved books and wished that one day she could carve out the time to sit down and write one herself. Meanwhile, more pressing things were on her page. She pulled herself away and headed for the reference desk where an elderly lady sat.

"Hi, I'm hoping you can help me with some research."

"I'll sure try," the librarian replied. "How can I assist you?"

"Well, there's this cold case. It's an incident that took place right here on the Main Line . . . the death of a little girl," Marly began. "You may remember it . . . Libby Kirshka?"

"Hmmm . . . " She tapped a finger on her lips.

"It happened Halloween night almost a decade ago or so."

The woman nodded. "Ah, yes. I think I do remember it. Shame they never solved that one."

"Yes, that's why I'm intrigued."

"Do you need to see any particular periodical?"

"*The Philadelphia Inquirer*, definitely, and, if possible, *Philadelphia Daily News*."

"Yep, we have them both." She gestured behind her. "We have microfilm or if you prefer digital resources, we have *NewsBank*."

"Oh, that's great . . . whatever."

"Do you know the year of the incident?"

"I'm thinking around 2016?"

"Microfilm or digital?"

"Um . . . let's do it old school. Microfilm is fine."

"Okay,"—she waved a hand—"come with me, dear, I'll get you set up."

****

Marly threaded the microfilm machine as the reference librarian instructed. While she cranked the handle, the fine print of newspaper articles, ads, and photos flashed, and memories surfaced from the last time she had to do this kind of research for a school assignment. She also recalled that scrolling too fast was a recipe for a headache. Putting the thought aside, she psyched herself up for the project. This wasn't some extra credit school assignment; this was her life.

The tiny print whizzed by fast as she searched for anything germane to the Halloween incident. After a while, her eyes strained from scrolling through the blur of text, and she slowed the momentum to avoid getting dizzy. Close to the end of the reel, something caught her attention. She scrolled back. There it was . . . exactly what she was looking for: "CHILD DIES IN CREEK BED." And then she found two more on the second reel: "GIRL, 6, DEAD BEHIND GLADWYNE HOME" and "CHILD DROWNS HALLOWEEN NIGHT."

Marly curiously scrolled through each of the stories. Surprised at seeing the street name, *Millbank Road*, where the incident apparently occurred, she shivered at the thought of the crime happening so close to her childhood home. After reading enough, she gathered the copies she made of the articles and returned the reels to the reference desk. Now, the real investigative work needed to be done.

Chapter Four

"Hello?"

"Hey, there."

"Hey, Dee."

"Thought I'd check in to see how you were feeling these days. Hope it's not too early."

"No, no. It's fine."

"You sound depressed."

"I'm okay," Marly fibbed. She struggled out of the bed covers to sit up. "Well, maybe a little."

"You have every reason to be. I would be, too, if I'd lost my job. It's only natural."

"I'm keeping busy, but I can't believe I got let go right in the middle of the hot story I was pursuing."

"I'm so sorry, hon. Life sucks sometimes."

"Tell me about it. Craig suggested I get some counseling. He's worried I'll end up drinking too much." Marly's thoughts quickly turned to sangria, and she wondered whether there was another bottle left downstairs.

"I'm sure you're not going to turn into an alcoholic. But there's no harm talking to someone. I highly recommend Dr. Kingsley if you ever decide to go that route. Talking things out is cathartic."

"Yeah, I've had my share of counseling after heartbreaks back in the day."

"Well, now, you've broken up with a job. Still hurts, right?"

Marly silently agreed. *Maybe it's time to get some talk therapy. Better than drinking.*

"You're *not* drinking too much, right?"

How does she know everything?

Dee sighed. "Sorry, my boss just texted me. Gotta run . . . have to take care of something for him."

"You always do." Marly chuckled. "I'm sure it's urgent."

"It's always something. Sometimes, I wonder who's running his business—me or him?"

"Well, we both know *you* are."

"Pffft, show me the money, right? Hey, call me later if you need anything."

"Sounds good. Thanks for checking in."

****

Marly dragged herself to the kitchen. The depression that engulfed her was nothing in particular, yet everything in general. Her job loss only punctuated her mental situation, and the reality now reared its ugly head, poking into her sensibilities. She'd confided in Dee over the years, but friends can only hear so much before growing a numb ear. And not everything could be shared with a friend. Some thoughts were too private.

Marly stood in the kitchen and stared out the window. In her heart, she knew that speaking to someone would be a good thing. She was approaching thirty, just lost her job and, of course, there's the private emotional matter she'd always kept to herself and probably always would because no one would understand. How much to reveal to a stranger gave her pause, but something needed to break, and the yet unopened bottle of sangria sparkling in the morning light on the countertop looked very tempting.

Chapter Five

THREE WEEKS LATER . . .

As Marly navigated through the medical complex, a red-brick building surrounded by thick oak trees came into view. A cluster of ivy resembling a thick green arm crept up the side and appeared to be reaching into a window. Seeing it reminded her of a horror film where medical experiments went awry, turning patients into zombies. Visiting a psychologist was one thing, but feeling like the next step might entail some kind of medical trial gave her pause. She had a fleeting thought to just turn around and drive back home.

The sign on the lawn in front of the building read #15. Marly parked the car, got out and headed for the steps leading up to the building. She pressed the buzzer and stood for a long minute staring at the weathered green door. It begged for a fresh coat of paint. When the door finally opened, a tall woman appeared wearing a white lab coat. She nodded and silently beckoned Marly inside. After taking only a few steps into the room, Marly startled at the sound of a metallic clink behind her. The woman in the lab coat had deadbolted the door.

What's going on here?

Marly's mind raced with intrusive thoughts. She tried not to be outwardly phased by the creepy feeling that came over her and kept her cool as best as she could. A knot twisted in her gut.

Does this person know I'm just here to visit a psychologist? Do I look insane? Already the pale lime green walls drew in closer as her pulse ticked up.

"I'm here to see Dr. Kingsley," Marly began, trying to maintain her composure. "Dr. Claire Kingsley."

The woman's brow crinkled as she shook her head. "There's no Dr. Kingsley here."

Marly's stomach dropped. *No Dr. Kingsley?* This was becoming more sinister by the minute. "There's no Claire Kingsley here? She's a psychologist."

The woman's pointed expression slowly softened. "Oh, I'm sorry, but you're in the wrong building." The tall woman strode over to the door and unlocked it. "You're in the psychiatric unit. You need to go across campus"—she pointed in the general direction as she fumbled with the key. "You want building number fifty-one. This is fifteen."

The tension in Marly's gut immediately released. Relieved that she wasn't going to be institutionalized and feeling a bit silly for mixing up the building numbers, a sense of lightness returned. *Am I dyslexic?* Even if she were, it paled in comparison to being mentally disturbed enough to have to be detained there, and it wouldn't be the worst thing that could have happened to her today. No, there were worse things.

****

A fish tank glowing in purple light sat in the waiting room of Dr. Kingsley's office. A large picture window held a crystal suncatcher pendant that cast a spectrum of rainbow colors over the walls through the sunlight streaming through. An air purifying machine hummed softly in the background. If the room could speak, it would say, *relax.*

"Dr. Kingsley's office, can you hold please?" a red-headed woman spoke into the phone. She glanced up. "Yes?"

"Hi, I'm doctor's three o'clock . . . Marly Maines."

"I'll need to see your insurance information. Are you a first-time patient?"

"I am."

Marly soon recognized the woman behind the desk. The last time Marly had seen Dee's cousin, Jen, was at a party earlier that summer at Ethan's house. She had been flirting with just about every guy there, including Ethan, and the exchange was painful to watch. She seemed to be trying too hard while the alcohol she'd been drinking didn't help. *Poor girl.*

"I'll need you to fill this out and sign it for me—front and back." She put a clip board on the counter. "By the way, I think I know you."

Marly felt her cheeks flush. "Yes . . . um, you're Dee's cousin, right?"

Jen nodded. "Yeah, I thought you looked familiar. I remember you from the party at Ethan's."

"Yes, small world, right?" Marly replied, nodding in sync with her. *When you were making a fool of yourself to get male attention.* Marly lent a cursory smile and stepped toward the seat at the window with the clipboard in hand.

While filling out the paperwork, doubt crept in. She knew that airing the thoughts and grievances pressing on her mind would be cathartic, but what if these sessions led to a dependency? She hated the idea of wasting her time—and her money—and didn't relish that Dee's cousin, of all people, would know of her need for a shrink. She'd prefer her business remain private.

*** *

Session:

Dr. Kingsley: So, what brings you here today? I see you've checked off drinking—let's see—more than two drinks per week. Is that the issue?

Marly: Well, first off, I'm not an alcoholic. Though sometimes I wonder. But I do drink, yes. It takes the edge off.

Dr. Kingsley: I see.

Marly: Besides, there's benefits to drinking, I've heard.

Dr. Kingsley: Oh?

Marly: Yes, in fact, staving off memory loss and certain types of cancer. There's lots of antioxidants in red wine.

Dr. Kingsley: Yes, so I've heard. But we're here to talk about why you feel the need to drink, not the benefits. Am I right?

Marly: Okay, yes, you're right.

Dr. Kingsley: So, please talk to me about what's concerning you most. No one is forcing you to reveal that which you don't want to say. I'm here for you. There's no pressure.

Marly squirmed. This could get awkward. So many things. She didn't know where to start. Though with the encouraging words from the doctor, Marly settled back and opened her heart. All that had been troubling her—the loss of her job, her inability to conceive, her emotions . . . just about everything came tumbling out over the next hour. Even more than she'd planned to say managed to escape her lips. Afterward, she felt a bit lighter from unloading so much. The weight of her initial doubts about the session subsided, and she was glad she came.

****

"Doctor?" Jen peeked her head inside her boss's office. "Tomorrow's 8 am cancelled—Mr. Dorman."

"Okay, thanks." Claire frowned. "Oh, these copies . . . "

"Everything alright?"

"These aren't good . . . "—she held up a piece of paper—"they're just not as dark as I'd like them to be."

"It's the toner. I'll change the cartridge. I'm pretty sure there's still one left."

"Oh, you're a dear." She tossed the sheet into the trash bin. "Yes, if you wouldn't mind. I've got to head out soon."

Before Jen left for the day, she retrieved the last remaining toner cartridge in the supply closet and installed it into her boss's printer. She waited a moment to run a quality control test copy. Examining it, the print looked perfect. Her boss would be pleased. Afterward, she straightened up the office, tossed an empty coffee cup, and noticed the discarded copies on the table that had not met her boss's approval. Something caught her eye. The copies were pale, sure, but she could still make out some of the words. A closer look at the transcript revealed something intriguing, and while drawn in, she fought the sense that it wasn't right to be reading the confidential material. It wasn't kosher; in fact, it was in violation of patient-doctor privacy, but after the first innocent glance, she couldn't resist being drawn into the text. Her curiosity had gotten the better of her when she saw a familiar name. She tried to make out the context of what was said, and her face flushed at what she read.

Chapter Six

ON THE WAY HOME from seeing the doctor, Marly reflected on the visit and wondered how long before the heavy veil of depression would lift. Gathering strength to do anything more than the bare minimum was exhausting, lately, and she'd let a number things—dusting, vacuuming, errands—go by the wayside. Still down from losing the best job she ever had, licking her wounds became her latest pastime and was her only solace, for now.

At the approach to the enclave of upscale stores just ahead, she spotted the sign for Tara's Café. Needing a caffeine jolt, she pulled in. The café always held a peaceful ambiance—so unlike the local Starbucks with its frenzied energy.

Marly stepped inside the quiet establishment and immediately felt drawn into another world. "I'll take a double espresso with cream, please."

While waiting for the order to be filled, she checked her phone for any messages. A few people occupied the small interior that held a few cozy tables. In the corner by the window, a familiar person sat alone in a booth.

"Hey, there!" she called out with a wave of her hand.

Ethan looked up from his laptop. He always brightened whenever he saw her. If he were a canine, his tail would be wagging. "Hey, Marly." His grin went all the way to his eyes. He was quite adorable she'd always thought and had known him forever . . . mainly, through Craig who'd been a frat brother in college.

"So, what are the odds?" she said, slipping into the seat across from him. "You just get off work?"

"Yeah,"—he gestured out the window—"had to pick up some stuff at Habitat for Humanity for my dad."

"By the way, how is he?"

"Good days and bad, I guess . . . " Ethan shrugged and began to describe his dad's progress after a recent fall. "He's got a way to go."

"Well progress is progress, right? At least there's that. Glad to hear it." She sipped her espresso. "Hey, listen,"—she patted his arm—"I'm glad I caught up with you because I wanted you to know something."

Ethan quirked an eyebrow.

"So, I was talking with Dee, and I think I know what she's hoping for . . . for Christmas, that is."

He held her gaze for a moment as he chugged his drink. "Oh, and what might that be?"

Marly smiled and held up her left hand. "A *ring*."

Ethan smirked.

"What? What's wrong with a ring?"

"Marly, I don't think so."

"You don't think what, exactly? You can't afford a ring? C'mon, dude, you've got a decent job. We know what the police department pays, even for a rookie cop. And you're no rookie." She slapped his arm.

"No comment," he replied, glancing toward the window. In the light of the late afternoon sun, his eyes shone as his gaze went back to her. "FYI, I'm with the fire department."

"Same thing. You rescue people, right?"

"Right." He nodded, rolling his eyes.

"So, you guys have been together for . . . what, ten years . . . eleven?" She took a long sip of the espresso.

He chugged the last of his drink. "Marly, I'm not the marrying kind of guy."

She waved her hand, dismissively. "Oh, Ethan, I don't believe that for a minute."

"It's true," he confessed, holding both palms up.

"Whatever." She didn't understand why this guy had cold feet. "But, hey, sorry . . . it's really not my business . . . so, please pardon my intrusion."

"You mean inquisition?"

"Ha, ha."

Ethan gave her his trademark smile, and they continued to chat for a good while. Eventually, Marly noticed the time. With that, she stood.

"Well, I think I'll go now. I need to stop at the store." She gulped the rest of the cup before tossing it into the trash receptacle.

"Guess I should be going, too." He closed his laptop.

As they walked out of the café, Marly pointed toward the end of the row of stores.

"Look!" She waved him on. "C'mere, let me show you something." At the approach to the last store, she turned to him with a mock grin on her face. "Now, I just want you to get familiar with the merchandise inside here." She pulled his arm and pushed him closer to the front window of a jewelry store.

"Okay, okay. Yeah, I get it."

"Those are *rings*," Marly said with emphasis. "They can't hurt you, and it would mean so much to your girl . . . you know, my oldest and dearest friend, Dee."

Ethan stared into the window.

"So, you'll think about it?"

"Hey, I get less pressure from Dee."

"Sorry. Just lookin' out for my girlfriend is all."

Ethan nodded. "I'm sure you are, but . . . "

"Don't say it." She held a finger to his lips. "Just think about it."

Ethan stared at the jewelry in the display window. After a moment, he turned to her. "I guess you want to pick out the ring for me, is that it?"

Marly chuckled. "No, no. That's *your job*." She slapped his arm.

Ethan nodded. "Got it . . . well, I've seen enough."

"Found what you like?"

"Marly," he said, his tone affectionately firm.

"Okay, okay. I've said enough, I know. Thanks for indulging me."

Before they parted, he reached out to hug her. "It was good to see you, kiddo."

"It was." She smiled as she looked up at him. "Okay, well, see ya, Ethan," she called back after stepping away, raising a hand to wave as she scampered toward the grocery store.

Chapter Seven

"Hello?"

"Hey."

"Hey, hon. What's up? On your way?"

"Still at work. Where are you?"

"Just got finished grocery shopping . . . on my way home now."

"Listen, I'm running late with a client, so don't make me anything for dinner. I'll probably have to take this one out to seal the deal."

"Oh, Craig . . . well, okay."

"I'll make it up to you."

"Promise?"

"Of course."

"Alright, but I'm holding you to it."

"Okay, gotta run."

"Love you."

At the traffic light, Marly turned on the radio. Her attention drew to a news story, and she paused at hearing the familiar voice. It was her former colleague, Christine Kirsh. Marly chafed at hearing the woman's voice. At this very hour was the time Marly once had been on the air. She didn't want to feel envious but couldn't help the hurt feeling that stabbed deeply. It just didn't make sense that she was let go. With all the others who could have been laid off, it still bothered her that she'd been the one whose head rolled. In the middle of the news report, she abruptly turned off the radio.

While waiting at the light, she noticed Millbank Road up ahead at the next intersection. Once again, the cold case came to mind, and the little girl's face flashed in Marly's head. The scene of the crime wasn't far from her present location. When the light turned green, she made a quick decision. Instead of going straight home, she turned right onto Millbank Road.

Marly drove along the shady, tree-lined street admiring the grand homes, one just as impressive as the next. The road curved and twisted downhill for most of the way. At one point, water from the nearby creek spilled across the roadway. She braked and took the drive slowly, knowing vehicles could lose traction and be swept away or even become submerged after a heavy rainfall. *Did it really only take four inches of water?*

Farther down the road, she slowed her speed again around the curving bend. After the next hairpin turn, a couple of prominent black mailboxes with gold lettering attracted her attention. The creek ran along the front of the nearby properties. On impulse, she pulled over. She wasn't sure what could be accomplished by getting out of the car, but something drew her to stop.

Marly opened the door and stepped out, careful to not slip on the smooth wet stones scattered on the driveway. Water puddled a few yards onto the properties and flowed between two homes— a stately Tudor and a glorified two-story cottage. Both residences resembled pages out of *Better Homes and Gardens* magazine.

She stepped gingerly along the gurgling creek, crossing onto the cottage property. *Marly, what are you doing? This is ridiculous. This is trespassing. Just leave now before a dog jumps out—or worse.* Despite the self-admonishing thoughts flitting through her head, she felt drawn as though by an invisible thread and kept walking, focused on her mission. In mid-stride, she glanced up at the cottage, hoping there weren't any eyes watching at the windows.

Around the side, a large paver patio spread almost the entire length of the home. She crept past the patio to the creek at the other end that trickled through a muddy patch of rocks and stones. The yard abutted to another home whose property aligned with the creek. *Was this where Libby fell? Who would have the animosity to harm a little child?* Marly stared at the water in a silent vigil in honor of the dead girl whose death, much like the famous unsolved crime involving JonBenét Ramsey, may always remain a mystery.

As nightfall began to close in, she turned back. For now, there was nothing more to see as imposing trees cast deep shadows in the yard. She was satisfied to have come this far, at least as a witness to the scene and observe in 3-D what may have happened—if, indeed, this was the actual scene.

While walking back across the lawn and onto the driveway, her senses spiked. Something felt odd. Her eyes darted to the patio where she sensed movement. Not breaking stride to pause, she held her breath and kept moving. *You're almost there, keep going . . . you'll make it . . . just a few more steps.* Then her worst fears came to life when a shadow emerged out of nowhere, and behind it, a figure loomed.

Chapter Eight

"Hello?"

"Dee, It's me."

"Hey, Jen."

"Just calling about our plans tonight. We still on?"

"Yeah, I'm still good."

"Wanna do the mall?"

"Perfect."

"Bertucci's okay?"

"Sure, sounds great."

"Good, I'll see you at five-thirty. Oh, while I have you, gotta tell you about something that happened today."

"What?"

"It was strange."

"Did something bad happen to you?"

"No, not to me. But you won't like it."

"Who then . . . what won't I like?"

"Y'know, on second thought, I think it's better that I tell you in person. I'll tell you later."

"You sure?"

"Yeah, in person is better."

"Okay, whatever. See you soon then."

****

Marly's nerves tensed upon seeing the shadow move.

"May I help you?" came the abrupt voice. At the command-ing tone, Marly froze, chagrined at being caught where she didn't belong.

"I'm sorry, I know I shouldn't be trespassing on your prop-erty, but I'm not an intruder or anything." She swallowed hard.

The imposing shadow shone a beam of light between the tall arborvitae trees surrounding the patio that landed directly onto Marly's face. The voice sounded like an older woman; the flash-light shook in her hand. At that, Marly let her guard down a bit in knowing the woman probably wasn't going to harm her unless, of course, the woman had a gun. *Did she?*

"What are you doing here?"

Marly held up her hand to block the piercing light. "My name is Marly Maines. I'm a reporter. I'm interested in what happened to a little girl named Libby Kirshka. She died under suspicious circumstances about nine years ago right in this neighborhood"—she gestured toward the creek—"where it was documented in the archived materials I got from the library. I'm investigating the in-cident. So, I . . . um, I was just curious if anyone around here knew anything or could give me any information?"

Stillness rose between them. The woman seemed reticent to answer. Marly held her breath. While she could have been ar-rested for boldly accessing the woman's property, this was more of a blessing—at least so far.

"Can you help me or do you have any information?" Marly hoped this would be her last question. She didn't want to badger the poor woman.

"I know all about what happened," the woman responded in a low voice while still holding the flashlight in Marly's face.

"How do you know?"

"I know because I was there."

Chapter Nine

DEE PERUSED THE DINNER menu while waiting for Jen. She settled on a personal-sized pizza with hot and sweet peppers and closed the menu just as Jen entered the restaurant. Dee held her hand up to wave.

"Hey,"—Jen slipped into the booth—"sorry I'm late."

"It's all good." Dee handed her a menu. "I'm getting pizza."

The scent of simmering tomato sauce and baking bread wafted by the table.

Jen took a cursory glance at the menu and then closed it. "I think I'll get that, too."

After giving the waitress their orders, Dee wondered when Jen was going to reveal what was on her mind regarding the cryptic conversation earlier. *What was she so eager to confess?*

With Dee's cousin, it was anyone's guess as to what could have piqued her interest. She'd always been a loose cannon in her growing up years. Still single at twenty-nine with a broken engagement—the closest thing to marriage for her thus far—Jen still held out for the right guy to come along, but Dee wondered who could tame this wild girl? She'd been a handful growing up, and her wild side needed something to assuage it, for sure.

"So, what's going on . . . is there something you wanted to tell me?" Dee asked after the waitress brought their orders.

"Um . . . " Jen pulled a clump of loose cheese hanging off the pizza and plopped it into her mouth. "Yeah, it was someone I saw." She picked up the napkin and wiped her mouth. "Rather, it's *something* I saw."

"Yeah?"

"It was Ethan. He was with your friend, Marly."

"You saw them together?"

"Yep."

"Hanging together?"

"Uh huh."

Dee's ears flushed. "Where was this?"

"At the café . . . that little place on Lancaster Avenue."

"Tara's?"

"Uh huh. They were sitting together in a booth and chatting."

"So, okay."

"They looked kind of cozy together."

"Are you saying they were holding hands or something?"

"No, but."

"But what?" Dee shrugged. "I'm not worried." Though at the same time, her stomach cinched.

"You're not worried?"

"Should I be? Marly's my oldest and dearest friend." She waved her hand as though dismissing the whole subject.

"Nothing to see there, right?" Jen asked with a tone of sarcasm.

"Jen, they've been friends for years. Her husband and Ethan are buddies since their school days. What of it?"

"Look, Dee, I'm not saying anything was going on, but there was just . . . I guess something in the air."

"A vibe?"

"Exactly. A vibe. But the part that bothered me the most was when I saw them walking out of the café and down to the jewelry store."

"Where were you?"

"In the parking lot."

"You were stalking them?"

"No, no. I'd just pulled up to the shopping center. Totally by chance. I spotted them through the window sitting at Tara's while I was in the car, and then I saw them leave together and walk down to the jewelry store. I guess I should have snapped a picture. But I think your friend is more than just a friend to Ethan."

"How's that? I mean, how do you know?"

"I think they like each other."

"So, what are you saying?"

"I think they're having an affair."

"Marly and Ethan?"

Jen nodded. "Sure. Didn't you tell me he's always bringing her name up in conversation? And the way he flirts with her. Oh, and didn't he buy her something for her car?"

Bile rose in Dee's throat. It all seemed so innocuous on the surface. Or could Jen have stumbled onto something? Dee processed the situation as nothing-to-see-here, but the subsequent visit to the jewelry store had her flummoxed.

"I wonder what they were doing at the jewelry store?"

"They didn't go inside, just stood outside looking in the window."

"Well, there's any number of reasons why they went there, right? Seems pretty harmless to me."

"Right." Jen smirked.

"What's that mean?"

"Never mind."

"I'm not worried about it, Jen. She's happily married *and* my best friend."

"She couldn't be stealing your man, right?"

"Jen, that's a terrible accusation. What's she done to make you so against her? I don't know what to say except what I said before. It doesn't bother me."

The moment the words left Dee's lips, the more she became curious. She put a spin on it to mask her insecurity, but she was forced to confront the facts. Could Jen's accusations be true? Did she even know her best friend at all?

"Sorry, I brought it up, Dee. I have my reasons. I just wanted you to know that I thought it looked odd is all."

Her reasons?

"I appreciate your looking out for me, but I trust my friend and my boyfriend."

"Well, when is he going to be more than just your boyfriend? How many more years does a girl have to wait?"

The question stung. Dee shook her head. "I don't think Ethan wants to get married."

"Do *you* want to?"

"Well, I've thought about it and hoped that maybe one day."

"When you're seventy? C'mon, Dee. You're not getting any younger. Besides, you do everything for him—cook, clean, I mean what else does a wife do that you don't?"

Dee bit her lip. Her mind spun with conflicting emotions. She didn't know how to process the info. Jen had a point, but Dee would not let on her true state of mind. No, Jen would come down on her even harder. She'd always been the bossier of the two while growing up, even though Dee was older. It seemed Jen had a more sophisticated POV, even at thirteen-years-old. She knew how to dress better than any of her peers and seemed light years ahead of them in every way—even as much as her intuition. So, was she correct now? Dee didn't want to believe it. Of course, Ethan would be faithful to her, and Marly was as close as a sister and would never betray anyone that way. *Would she?*

Chapter Ten

MARLY'S JAW DROPPED AT hearing the woman's words, amazed at the serendipity of the moment. The woman stared into the distance, seeming to recollect her thoughts.

"You were there?"

"I was in my house—not far from where it happened. But I heard it—a scream. It was so long ago, but I remember hearing a piercing scream. I thought it came from down by the creek since the water carries sound. I figured that had to be where it was coming from. I looked out the window"—she shook her head—"but I couldn't see anything . . . just heard a frantic voice. It was awful."

"Did you call the police?"

"No. I just froze. I wanted to run outside, but I wasn't dressed and, well, I was afraid. And then not long afterward, there was an ambulance and a cop car at the scene . . . flashing lights and everything."

"The newspapers said they found her in the creek," Marly said. "And the police reports stated there were some marijuana cigarettes floating in the water."

"You know, I saw something," she began in a whisper. "One particular night." She pointed toward the creek. "My neighbors have a son. He's long graduated from school now, but when he was living there, I went to their house to give Beth, his mother, some flowers from my garden when she'd been ill. Anyway, while standing at the door, I noticed something in the bushes. It looked like a rolled-up cigarette."

"Marijuana?"

The woman nodded. "I'm sure that kid was a dealer."

"How do you know?"

"How could I not? People coming and going all the time and not staying long. Whenever I walked my dog at night, I saw a blue light on in the window. Back in my day when a kid in my school was selling, he put a light in his window." She pursed her lips. "The smartest kid in the school . . . so polite yet doing drugs. Had everyone fooled." She shrugged. "Can't figure people out for nothing, I guess."

"Hmmm . . . this sheds some new light for sure. It's just so odd that no one has been implicated in this case."

A ghost of smile rose on the old woman's lips for a moment. "Well, no one knows for sure who was with the child the night she died, but . . . "

"But?"

The woman sighed. "There's nothing I can prove, but I have a feeling I know who was responsible."

"You never wanted to speak up to the police or report it?"

"I did. But they probably just considered it hearsay. Besides, the police did a thorough investigation, questioned the whole neighborhood and still . . . "

"You have a feeling you know who it is?"

"Just my gut sense." She slowly shook her head. "But there's no way the perpetrator would be identified, let alone punished."

"How's that?"

"Because of his parents' influence . . . especially, his father."

"Who was his father?"

"Local bigshot in Philadelphia."

Local bigshot? Did he live nearby?

Marly hung on the woman's every word even though her head began to throb with a migraine. She had more questions to ask, but the pressure was making her lightheaded. As much as Marly found the story intriguing, she needed something to quench the pain. In

32

addition, her husband may already be home by now. He might be worried where she was, and the frozen food sitting in the car was probably beginning to defrost. Although there was more to ask, it was best to get back to her car. She'd gotten a good lead, and it was enough for now, but she would come back.

"Listen, I should go now. I appreciate your help . . . thank you so much Ms.?"

"Muriel," the woman replied.

"I'm so grateful to you, Muriel," Marly began. "After all, you could have had me arrested."

"You're too pretty to have arrested. But it's a good thing my sweet Silky Sue isn't here or she'd have barked you right off the property."

Thank God for small favors. "Cute name. What breed is she?"

"She was a Springer Spaniel. She went over the rainbow bridge last year."

"Oh, no. I'm so sorry to hear that."

"It's what pets do. They leave you."

"I feel your pain . . . I do." Marly paused. "Well, I should be going. Thanks, again, for the information. You've been a great help to me." She turned to leave but hesitated. Her curiosity pressed in. "Muriel, just one more question for you."

"Yes?"

"The neighbor you speak of—the parents of the boy—do they still live in the neighborhood?"

"I'm afraid the wife died, and the son moved away. But the father still lives there." She nodded toward the adjacent property.

"There?" Marly pointed to the Tudor home.

Muriel nodded.

Marly's determination to find justice for Libby grew even more. The fact that someone could be culpable or potentially covering up for a wayward son gave her the courage to pursue things even further. If anything, this person needed to come to terms with the situation and, hopefully, pay what was due to the little girl's family. He owed it to society and mostly to himself whether he realized it or not.

As Marly walked back down the driveway between the two homes, she mused on what Muriel mentioned. She wanted to knock on the man's door right then and there but thought it better to approach during the day rather than at night.

While pulling out onto the road, she glanced back at the mailbox on the other side of the driveway from Muriel's. She tried to make out the name stenciled on the side. Then the abrupt blare of a car horn startled her as an oncoming vehicle came barreling up the road. She slammed her foot hard on the brakes and braced for impact. Miraculously, the driver's car ended up stopping mere inches from her own.

"Are you okay?" the driver called out as he hurried toward her.

"Yeah, I think so." Adrenaline pulsed through her body causing her head to throb even more.

"Sorry about that."

"No, it was my fault. I was distracted."

He frowned. "Actually, I was speeding."

"No harm done, just to my blood pressure is all."

The man stared at her. At one point his eyes lit up. "You look familiar."

Marly understood where this was going. She got it all the time. "I'm Marly Maines."

"Oh, wow," the man exclaimed. "I'm so sorry—"

"No, it was my fault, sir. I wasn't watching where I was going. Stupid mistake."

"You sure you're alright?"

She nodded. "I'm okay. Appreciate your concern."

The man stood staring at her and waited a moment before going back to his car. After he left, Marly sighed and started the engine again. Before pulling away, she glanced over at the mailbox that drew her attention earlier. In the light of the street lamp, she was taken aback, perplexed at what she saw. There was only one person who fit the bill of whom Muriel described. The name on the mailbox confirmed it. Although the letters had been worn, there was no mistaking what it spelled. *Strauss.*

Could it be John Strauss? VP of MNN? A shiver ran through her.

Chapter Eleven

DEE DROVE TO ETHAN's house after dining with Jen. As much as she wanted to clear the air with him, something gave her pause. She knew he wouldn't be home tonight because of working a double shift. So, it would be a good time to get some uninterrupted housecleaning done. In the interim, she had time to reflect on her situation in light of what Jen had mentioned earlier. If she couldn't talk to him immediately, the next best thing would be to carry on despite the emotional pain and disillusionment. An opportunity to exercise some emotional intelligence instead of flailing and going off on him would help the situation. After all, who knew whether Jen was telling the truth or just some imaginative scenario fabricated from her overactive mind.

Dee started a load of laundry and popped a shepherd's pie into the oven for him to reheat later. Then she began vacuuming the downstairs of his two-story clapboard. Cleaning for him had become routine for as long as she could remember, and multi-tasking was her thing. Being a bachelor, he wasn't the tidiest of persons. His lackluster sense of order annoyed her so much that one day she just took it upon herself to do the cleaning for him. It was easier than arguing. After vacuuming, she gave the downstairs furniture a thorough wiping down. Thankfully, Ethan's dog was no longer around to contribute to the mess. While she missed Poncho, she didn't at all miss the dog hair clinging to everything. The upstairs didn't need much except the stripping of the bed and a quick dusting of the bureau, armoire, end tables, and the headboard. Seeing the fingerprints on the headboard annoyed her. She used polish to get the surface clean. Later, after the wash and dry cycles finished, she brought the clean laundry up to his room.

As Dee climbed the stairs, her cousin Jen's words floated in her mind, haunting her since their talk at the restaurant. *Dee, what do you do for him that a wife doesn't?* Dee didn't have an answer; the true answer being *nothing.* There was no difference between a wife and her place as his girlfriend. She'd been in the role for over eleven years, but what had she earned from it? There was no ring and no promise for the future. Better question: What had she learned? The more she pondered, the more insecure she became. Without reassurance, what was the point of the relationship? Was he happy in the situation, or just playing a habitual role? The lack of an engagement ring or even a friendship ring spoke volumes. He'd been married before. So, what was wrong with getting married a second time?

Dee unloaded the laundry basket and mentally rehearsed what she'd say to him when he got home. She folded the towels and placed them in the linen closet and put the rest of his clothes inside his closet and drawers. Afterward, she carried the two upstairs trash cans down to the kitchen. As she emptied the contents into the garbage bin under the sink, she noticed a torn piece of paper with letterhead on it. Curious, she reached in and pulled out the other pieces. After putting it together like a puzzle, it appeared to be a letter addressed to Ethan from a doctor's office. Struck by what she read, the words took her aback. *This can't be true.*

Dee's heart raced. She bit her lip. The words, "terminal illness" from a doctor at Sacred Heart Hospital shook her to the core. She read and re-read the doctor's letter confirming the diagnosis of a particular type of cancer that was found, hoping her eyes deceived her. Her hands trembled. She wished by sheer willpower the words could be interpreted in some way to make the diagnosis less disheartening. The state of his health had been confirmed, the letter said, through numerous diagnostic tests and examinations. She stared until the words blurred. *No, this can't possibly be true.* Ethan hadn't mentioned his condition to her. He'd never said a word. The shock of reading this was too much. She sat down at the kitchen table and cried.

Chapter Twelve

"Hello?"

"Hi, deary," came the familiar voice.

"Aunt Muriel?"

"Hi, Chrissy. How are you doing sweetheart?"

"I'm good. How are you?"

"Can't complain. Hangin' in there, But I gotta tell ya, don't get old, Chrissy."

"I'll do my best," Christine said with a chuckle.

"Aging is not for the weak, that's for sure."

"Aunt Muriel, you'll always be young—at least at heart."

"Well, I'd like to think so. Anyway, I just wanted to reach out to you. Been thinking about you. And the reason I'm calling is that I must tell you something."

"Oh, I hope it's nothing serious . . . are you okay?"

"Yes, yes, I'm fine, dear. It's not about me."

"Phew. You had me worried there."

"Listen, a woman reporter was just in my backyard."

"What . . . who?"

"Yeah, a woman named Marly. She was here investigating what happened to Libby."

Christine froze. "Marly Maines? What did she say?"

"Just nosing around, asking the usual questions about that night and who may have been responsible."

"What did you tell her?"

"Of course, nothing. Nothing much, anyway."

Christine's guilt draped like a veil. She hadn't felt this way in a long time. The death of her younger sister was many years ago, but now the fangs of regret bore down and tore the protective layer of her heart that held the memories in check. Now, she felt exposed. She'd managed to climb out from behind the shadow where she hid—even as a young girl when she felt inadequate and never quite measuring up to the perfection her mother instilled. Sadly, her mother's vision for her first daughter never materialized. When Libby came along, the attention and grooming fell to her. A star was born. As a young girl, Christine thought her problem was Libby. Now, she knew differently, but it was too late. With both parents gone, she'd never be able to show them that she, too, became a star in her own right.

"I'm sorry to bring this up out of the blue, but I just thought you should be aware is all."

Shocked by the revelation, Christine felt at a loss for words but managed an *okay* in response. Though she was anything but okay. Her heart plummeted like a stone. Muriel was the only person Christine had ever confided in. Even so, she didn't reveal everything to her aunt. While she could have shared her entire heart, she reserved a part. Despite her reticence to keep some things hidden, Christine could tell her aunt was shrewd enough to see more than she let on.

The deep layers of protection that Christine had built over her heart were invisible to most people but not to Muriel. While her mother was busy doting on Libby, the only solace Christine found was in the arms of her aunt. They bonded over the years much like mother and daughter. Even without Christine's full disclosure, Muriel knew what happened, and yet she never judged nor said a word to anyone.

Chapter Thirteen

"HE'S DYING, MARLY," DEE sobbed into the phone.

"What? Who are you talking about?"

"Ethan."

"Oh, Dee, I can't believe it. How do you know?"

"Cancer. It's what I saw in some paperwork that I found in his trash can."

"Paperwork?"

"A diagnosis. From a doctor."

"I can't understand that, but yet again, I can. He just wants to protect you, probably."

"I guess. I don't know. He never mentioned anything to me— at all. He's been a bit withdrawn, lately. Not opening up as much as though something heavy was on his mind."

"I'm so sorry. Do you know what kind of cancer . . . what stage?"

"I don't know. I just found the papers. I haven't even been able to get ahold of him to ask him anything about it. I'm a mess."

"Oh, Dee. I just don't know what to say except hang in there. There are so many treatments for cancer these days. Just pray they've caught it in time."

"I know, but it still hurts."

"I'm sure. Listen, give it some time. There's all kinds of medical interventions today. You never know the future with these kinds of things. God is still in the miracle business, don't forget."

"I guess." Dee sniffled.

"It's true. He is, Dee. Just keep that in the forefront. You're going to be alright . . . things will be okay. By the way, did I tell you the latest on the case I'm investigating, the one I was working on when I got canned?"

"The Halloween story?"

"Uh huh. I spoke to a woman who was there the night it happened."

"Seriously?"

"Yeah. Lucky break. She gave me some information. So, we'll see how it goes. It's almost finished, just a few more details to work out."

"That's great. Are you still seeing Dr. Kingsley?"

"Yep. I'm finally able to open up to her. Poor woman hears it all from me now. God bless her."

"I'm so glad. You do sound much better. I guess we've switched roles."

"Oh, Dee. My heart goes out to you and Ethan. It really does. This must be so devastating for him. For you both."

"I just don't know what to do for him, especially when he gets in a down mood. But I understand now that it's probably the diagnosis. I'm just holding on loosely at this point."

With all that was on Dee's mind regarding Ethan's health, the sticky issue with Marly and Ethan didn't seem quite as important. Even if there were any truth in Jen's accusation, it paled in comparison to what Dee now faced in light of her boyfriend's mortality. While Dee had planned to address the topic with Marly, right now was not the time.

Chapter Fourteen

Two weeks later . . .

"Johnny? It's Mel, from *The Sentinel.*"

"Mel, good to hear from you. Been awhile. What do I owe you?"

"Ha, yeah. No, we're good, buddy. Hey, listen. It's come to my attention from one of my managing editors that there's a story here recently submitted. Seems it involves you."

"Me?"

"Your name is mentioned here."

"What did I do now?"

"Well..."

"Does it involve the school board?"

"No, not really."

"Then what?"

"Okay . . . let's see here. It's the cold case Halloween mystery."

"Halloween mystery?"

"Yep, involving the young girl who was found dead in Gladwyne."

"Oh, that story. Um, okay . . . well, how long ago was that? Well over a decade or so now, right?" He gave a short chuckle.

"Uh, not that long."

"Well, how much interest could there be now?"

"Young girl's death . . . cold case. It's always a hot topic, Johnny."

"Oh, okay. So how am I mentioned—or, better yet, why?"

"Seems like Marly Maines submitted the story . . . has quotes from neighbors. By the way, where do you live? Your family still on the Main Line?"

"Uh huh. Still live in Gladwyne, but my wife passed and it's just me now."

"That's rough. You have my condolences, buddy."

"Thanks, Mel."

"You bet'cha. Listen, I just wanted to give you a heads up about the story."

"Yeah, I do appreciate the call, Mel."

"Not a problem."

"Listen . . . uh . . . is it at all possible not to run the story?"

"Not run it?"

"Yeah."

"Oh, boy. Not sure." Mel snickered. "I mean, I could field it for you—"

"No, no. I don't want you to stick your neck out or anything."

"Any reason?"

"Full disclosure . . . I just don't want the publicity. With the school board and my job, things are already kind of touch-and-go. I'm just concerned for my reputation and—"

"Let me see what I can do, Johnny. Maybe I could have the story edited. Not sure but I'll try."

"That would be great, Mel. I'd really appreciate that. I'll definitely owe you for this."

"Okay, Johnny. We'll talk soon."

John hung up the phone. Dealing with slipping news ratings, along with personnel cuts and budgetary issues had stressed him. Now, his personal life was next on his list of troubles. Possibly, even his job could be on the line because of this story should his family's name be publicized again.

In the first version, years ago, he'd managed to get his son's name redacted. Now, with Marly Maines' talent as an investigative reporter, the buried details may not remain so hidden, especially since she'd cut ties with him the moment he'd let her go. She owed him nothing at this point, though it didn't sit well with him to be potentially exposed negatively with hearsay evidence about his family on that fateful night. There was too much at stake.

It was a known fact that Steve Strauss had been home the evening of Halloween and hadn't gone to election headquarters with the family to witness his father's victory in the race for school board President. It had been a sore spot between father and son. Instead, Steve had been in the vicinity of the creek where the little girl drowned. The police interviewed him and several others at the scene. There was no foul play—only that the little girl's paper bag contained candy that all spilled into the creek. There was evidence of some marijuana joints floating in the water between a few of the rocks in the creek bed. The only people in the immediate area were a few trick-or-treaters, including John's son, Steve. Even so, John Strauss was not so keen on having this story come out a second time. The association between drugs and his son's name was too hot a combination to attempt to defend again.

****

"Knock, knock." Christine stood at the threshold to John's office. "You alright?"

John pushed his chair back and stood as she entered. She walked across the room and wrapped her arms around her boss's waist. He pulled himself away and ran a hand through his hair.

"What's wrong, John?"

"The story. The Halloween night tragedy."

"My sister's story?"

He nodded. "The story Marly was working on before I let her go."

"Is there a problem?"

"Chris, I never wanted that piece to get an audience—no way, no how. It's incriminating. It's tragic. And my son was named at the scene or near it somehow, I don't remember. I've put it behind me.

44

All I know is that the publicity nearly cost me the election, and I lost my marriage over it after Beth got ill and then . . . " He hung his head. "Well, the marriage was already at the tipping point, but the incident just pushed it over the edge. I don't need any more aggravation—or reminders. The whole thing was brutal for all of us, and I don't want to relive it again."

"How do you know it's going to be published?"

"Got a call from one of my editor friends at *The Sentinel.*"

"Maybe it'll get bumped or something. Is there a chance it could?"

"I can't live with that pressure. Can't live with a *maybe.* I'd do anything to stop the presses on it."

"What are you going to do?"

"I've got to stop it from happening. It's the reason—well, not the only reason—but it's part of the reason I let her go in the first place."

"You fired her for—"

"No, she was scheduled to be laid off. Budget problems were the main reason, but . . . "

"I get it. Squelch the story?"

"Yep. And, of course, I couldn't let you go," he said, and pulled her toward him in a tight embrace.

"Hey, listen," Christine said. "What if the story hasn't really come out yet?"

"What do you mean?"

"I mean, the *real* story. Like what if all the details aren't quite what they appear? What if somebody missed something? Maybe, your son had been framed or something?"

"I don't think he was *framed*, exactly. He was just in the wrong place at the wrong time is all."

"Right, but what if the real story speaks otherwise?"

"I never thought of that as a possibility."

"There's always the chance that new details could come out, right?"

"You sound like you know something, or is this just some misguided hope of yours?"

"No, no. It's just . . . it's that I care." After a moment of silence, Christine stepped away and moved toward the door. With a wave she said, "I'll see you later. My shift starts soon."

"We still on for tonight?"

"Sure."

"Seven o'clock—our usual spot?"

"I'll be there."

She opened the door and stepped into the hallway leading to her studio. On her way down the hall, a rush of sorrow came over her and tears began to flow.

Chapter Fifteen

Session:

Dr. Kingsley: So, how are things going these days?

Marly: I guess okay.

Dr. Kingsley: Depression level?

Marly: Still a bit depressed.

Dr. Kingsley: There's light at the end of the tunnel, yes?

Marly: I'm trying to see it.

Dr. Kingsley: There always is a bright spot . . . that is, when you search for one. Now, at your own pace, let's talk about anything else on your mind, and then we can start some EMDR at some point if you'd like . . . see how that works for you.

Marly: I've heard of it.

Dr. Kingsley: It helps to desensitize any trauma by engaging the bilateral stimulation of the eyes.

Marly: Sounds interesting. I'd like to try that.

Dr. Kingsley: Absolutely. Though first, I have a protocol around it.

Marly: Protocol?

Dr. Kingsley: I'll need to get some more information from you first, and then we have to prep you for it. Could take another session or two for that.

Marly: Oh, okay. But after I'm prepped and all, how does it work?"

Dr. Kingsley: Well, you'll sit back, breath slowly, and track my hand movements with your eyes.

Marly: Kind of like a hypnotism?

Dr. Kingsley: Not exactly. But, yes, there's a rhythm to it. You'll see. Meantime, for today, tell me about what's been happening in your life since your layoff?

Marly: Well, let's see. Oh, I've got a pet investigative project underway.

Dr. Kingsley: Sounds like something germane to your skills.

Marly: It was my job for a good while. I'm hoping to get the story out again in front of the public. It's a cold case, but someone must know something. The last time anyone posted anything new was years ago. But I hope the resurrection of it will lend some fresh light and, possibly, a new investigation.

Dr. Kingsley: It sounds like this new project is working for you—in more ways than one, it seems.

Marly: Well, it's helped distract me from my funk a bit. I wish I had my old job back, but . . .

Dr. Kingsley: Seems this story may put you back on the radar among the news crowd. I'm sure the by-line will lend something and perhaps alert the powers that be at other news outlets.

Marly: I hope so. It would be great. I just want to be able to use my skills and talents in my field. It doesn't have to be on-air work. Writing for a paper or an online news outlet would serve me just as well.

Dr. Kingsley: Well, if I have any say in the matter, I think your past work speaks for itself. Frankly, I've been a fan of yours for years now.

Marly: Oh, doctor, thanks. That's too sweet. You have some fans, too, you know. You've come highly recommended by my friend, Dee, for one. So, I'm glad for this opportunity to unburden my load on you.

Dr. Kingsley: I'm here any time you need me.

Marly: It's so much better than holding all of these thoughts inside. I know I'm supposed to cast all of my cares on God, but sometimes, I just need to talk to a flesh-and-blood person. My husband has been great, but there's only so much I can tell him before he starts to feel like a girlfriend.

Dr. Kingsley: I understand. It's good that you reached out. We all benefit by airing our thoughts and feelings. Better than letting things fester.

Marly: Now that it's all out there, I hope there's no recrimination. Like I can't take it back now, right?

Dr. Kingsley: Oh, not to worry, Marly. Your secrets are safe with me. It's what I'm sworn to do.

Chapter Sixteen

A LITTLE AFTER SEVEN, John waited at the bar while nursing a glass of chardonnay. He kept an eye on his phone as well as the lobby of the restaurant, expecting Christine at any minute. She wasn't usually late, but Friday night traffic combined with pouring rain was almost a guarantee that lateness would trump a timely arrival. He fiddled with the napkin, folding and unfolding it as he drank. By the time he finished the glass, Christine arrived and headed toward the bar. He quickly signaled for another two glasses of wine.

"I was getting a little worried," he admitted, helping her take off her wet raincoat.

"Traffic."

"I'm sure. I ordered you a white wine."

"Thanks. I'll need it."

Christine slid onto the seat next to him as the bartender placed two glasses of wine in front of them. As she raised the rim to her lips, something about the moment felt a bit off. It was nothing obvious, a mere sensation. For now, he hoped it could be dismissed as his own paranoia. Emotions aren't facts, but he felt some distance with Christine. It was off-putting. When she put her glass down on the napkin and faced him, his stomach twinged.

"Seems like something's on your mind," John began. "Is everything okay?" He reached for his glass and took a long gulp.

Christine shook her head while lending a ghost of a smile.

"What is it, honey?" In the long silence between them, she seemed to have trouble looking him in the eye.

"I . . . I've had something to tell you for a long time, John."

John's stomach tightened. "I'm listening."

"It's . . . "

"Is it about us—you and me?"

"Oh, no. Not exactly, but . . . "

"But what, Chris? Just tell me." His anxiety climbed.

"Not here. Can we talk more privately?"

"Sure, let's find a table."

John paid the bill, and they moved to an empty booth. While sitting across from each other, John patted her hand.

"It's not pretty," Christine began.

"Hey, what's going on?"

"I don't even know where to start."

"Start at the beginning. My time is yours." He squeezed her hand, hoping it would reassure her that whatever was on her mind would be welcomed by him.

"Well, that would bring me back to my growing up years. I'm not sure you have that kind of time or patience to listen to my saga."

"I'm not going anywhere, Chris." He lent a stiff smile. "I'm listening."

"Like I said, it's not pretty, and it was a long time ago."

Chapter Seventeen

October 31
Halloween night
Nine years earlier . . .

Chrissy hated Halloween. Everything about the night chafed her sensibilities—witches, goblins, and ghosts. It was juvenile and not her type of entertainment. Hanging with her little sister, Libby, while the girl pranced through the neighborhood collecting sweets from well-meaning neighbors, was not her idea. Her mother had insisted.

"Her Halloween costume looks adorable, doesn't it?" Libby's mother primped her daughter's red wig, modeled after the movie character in *The Little Mermaid*. "Oh, Libby. You look so cute," her mother gushed. "Are you okay walking in the costume?"

"Mom, it's fine. I told you already." Libby bent over and touched her toes. "See? I'm good."

"But it's down to the ground . . . just be careful."

"She's *fine*, Mom." Chrissy crossed her arms and rolled her eyes at her mother's doting. "You worry too much."

The praising of Libby was nothing new, and this wasn't the first time Libby looked especially cute. She'd been deemed a beautiful child from day one. Everyone couldn't help but notice—especially Chrissy, who now existed in her sister's shadow. It would have been okay if people hadn't made such a fuss over Libby, or if there could have been reciprocity or equal affection shown toward the two sisters, but Chrissy always felt she took a back seat. It had been this way since Libby was born. Chrissy had become a surrogate caretaker at her mother's behest and went from childhood to nanny in a matter of a few years. Constantly under a directive to be there—for Libby. *Libby needs this . . . Libby needs that . . . Chrissy, please help your sister.* Everything was all about Libby.

****

"Where's the Halloween party?"

"Jake's house . . . we need to hurry."

"How much do you have?"

"Enough."

"How much did it cost?"

"Special deal. Just wrap 'em, Charlie. I'll explain later."

"We making spliffs or—?"

"No, just weed."

"You get this from Spunky?"

"Yeah. Better hurry. My parents will probably be home from the town council meeting any minute. If my dad didn't win the election, he's gonna be pissed, so . . . "

"I think I heard something. Someone's at the door."

"Probably trick-or-treaters."

"Sounded like the garage door opening."

"You sure? Crap, they're home. This isn't good."

"Don't panic, Strauss."

"Don't panic? Man, if my dad catches me with—"

"Hold on. I've got an idea."

"I need to hide this stuff."

"It'll be fine. Trust me."

****

"Okay, girls. Remember, don't stay out too long. Chrissy, please stay with Libby. Don't let her go off by herself. Keep an eye on her."

Chrissy inwardly balked. "Of course, Mom. I know." *And what if I don't?*

"Both eyes, please." She held her hands on her hips. "And make sure to only stop at the houses on this street. Just stay in the neighborhood. I don't want her coming home with any strange peoples' candy, and I'll be checking it before you eat any," she admonished.

"I know . . . just in the neighborhood," Chrissy repeated, flatly.

"And be back before dark."

"Got it."

"Is Jen going with you?"

"Yeah, she's meeting us at the curb—oh, there she is now. Hey, Jen! Be right out," Chrissy called from the doorway.

"Just be back before I start to worry."

"Chill, Mom. It's all good."

****

The town council meeting room thrummed. Among the buzz of high energy chatter, the air sizzled with anticipation while John Strauss paced in the wings. The odds of him winning the council's presidency again were in his favor, but newcomer, Chuck Spaulding, had been gaining momentum in the polls, according to the stats that recently came in. It wouldn't be the worst thing to lose, but the competitor in him needed the validation. He'd been in leadership for the past decade. He couldn't lose now. Though the pressure remained palpable as he waited for the voting results to be tallied. By 7 pm, most of the polls had already closed. Minutes later, cheers erupted in the room.

"John, looks like you've got this!" Andy, his campaign manager, slapped him on the back.

John let out a sigh. "It was close, I'm sure."

"We knew you'd win, buddy. We all did."

****

"Charlie?"

"Yeah?"

"Where's the rest?"

"The weed?"

"Yeah, the weed."

"Well, you said you needed to get rid of it, so . . . "

"So, where is it?"

He smirked. "You know those trick-or-treaters?"

"What about them?"

"Your parents were about to bust in on us. So, when I answered the door, I slipped it in one of the kid's bags, along with some candy bars sitting by the table."

"You *what?*" Steve's face flushed. "Tell me you didn't."

"We needed to get rid of it fast. You said so. So, that's what I did."

"You're an idiot!" Steve scrambled to the front door. "C'mon, Charlie. We gotta go get that stuff back."

"Sorry, buddy. I just didn't think, okay. It's barely a nickel bag anyway—"

"Wrong, man. It was more than that, but that's not the point here. Let's go."

Steve frantically hustled down the rear stairway and out the back door of the kitchen, narrowly avoiding his parents. He turned back to Charlie, who ambled down the lawn.

"Okay, whose bag, Charlie?"

"Whose bag?" Charlie ambled down the lawn.

"Yeah, whose bag did you dump it in?"

"Uh . . . I think it was a princess costume."

"You think?" You'd better know, Charlie."

"Yeah, probably princess or maybe a ballerina?"

"Oh, man, you are stupid."

"Sorry, I was too nervous to pay attention."

"Okay, like what color costume was it? Can you at least remember that?"

Charlie paused as he tried to recollect. "Um . . . uh."

"C'mon, man. Hurry up." Steve, now frantic, looked up and down the street. A couple of kids in costumes walked up the hill, and a few more across the street headed in the direction of the creek. "There's kids in both directions, and we're running out of light." He silently cursed his luck.

"I think a red wig. Yeah, it was a little kid with a red wig."

"A red wig?" He sighed in frustration. "Okay, long hair . . . short . . . what?"

"I-I don't know. It could be a kind of—"

"Oh, you're useless. I'm going this way." Steve hustled down the street, keeping his eye out for anything *red*.

Chapter Eighteen

"Oh, don't you look like a pretty little mermaid."

Libby grinned. "I'm Ariel."

"Yes, you are." The woman smiled and placed a handful of sourballs into her sack.

"Thank you," Libby called out as she scampered back across the lawn toward the street.

"Such delightful costumes," she said to the children as she doled out more candy. The child wearing a Frankenstein costume grunted something to her as he held open his sack wide. "Oh scary!" the woman replied with mock fright.

"Your little sister is so cute," a neighbor said of Libby as she walked past Chrissy and Jen. "Love her costume."

Chrissy smirked. "Yeah, she's adorable."

"So, back to Josh. Chrissy, what did he say, again? And what did he text you?"

"He kind of asked me out."

Jen lit up. "That's great."

"Well, he *kind* of did."

"So, what's that mean?"

"I just got the feeling that he was trying to—"

"He probably was!" shrieked Jen. "I *know* guys . . . he was for sure. He's a senior, right?"

"Yep. Obviously, he was shy about it . . . so, that's when I just—"

"Asked him yourself?"

"Ha, yeah." Chrissy giggled. "Well, almost."

"Hey, where's your sister?"

Chrissy looked up. "Oh. Yeah, I don't see her." She glanced around. "Hey, Libby!"

"Where'd she go?"

"I don't know. Don't worry, she's probably up the street by now. Or down." Chrissy glanced in every direction. There wasn't a trick-or-treater in sight, but she wasn't alarmed in the least.

****

"No, no, it's my candy . . . no, get off it," Libby shouted. A tall figure stood holding the edge of Libby's paper bag. "No, it's mine," she cried.

While they tussled over the sack, Chrissy overheard the shouting and went down to the edge of the creek to see what the scuffle was about.

"What are you doing?" Chrissy shouted at the figure. She recognized him as her neighbor; the boy she once babysat many summers ago had become a young man. It shocked her to witness the change in his looks—height, weight, and the hint of tiny hairs spiking on his chin. No longer a child, this boy-man towered over her. His expression bore a frightened look resembling a deer in headlights.

"I'm . . . I'm . . . I gotta get something—"

"Let it go," Chrissy demanded. "Let it go now, Stevie!"

As the tug-of-war continued between the two, Libby's bag ripped. Some of the contents spilled out into the creek.

"Oh, no!" Libby cried as pieces of candy plopped into the water and floated away in the pulsing current.

"Now, look what you've done," said Chrissy. In a matter of moments, she attempted to scramble onto the watery stones, determined to salvage the situation, but something came over her. An unexpected feeling churned inside. Amid her sister's screaming and while holding onto the handle of the sack, coupled with the boy's subsequent yanking on the other handle, Chrissy stood in between in an effort to separate them. Only Chrissy's intentions did not meet reality. In her forceful jerking of the handle, it pulled free in her hands, and somehow, Libby must have lost her balance as the next thing Chrissy saw was Libby in the creek. Chrissy, still holding the handle, watched the rest of the candy and contents of the bag float out into the current. A snaking red trickle slipped into the stream and pooled in the water around Libby's bloodied head. Her body—now limp—floated silently in the water before a current took her farther into the rushing stream.

Chrissy stood in shock at the sight of her sister in the water. "Libby!" she cried. Frozen with fear, her heart strained in her chest. The only other witnesses to what happened were her friend, Jen, who stood nearby, and Stevie Strauss—now a grown-up teenager, not her young charge. No longer the one she could tuck in bed and close the light or fib to him about whether there really was a Santa Claus and have him believe every word she said. No, he was wiser these days, almost an adult. Even though he'd grown up and was no longer a child, was he all-knowing, too? *Did he see what happened?* She didn't know whether he was able to observe everything. *Did anyone?* If not, she wouldn't have to admit that she didn't try to help her sister. While Chrissy hadn't planned to harm the child, the rocky creek did it for her.

****

Libby Kirshka was pronounced dead in the early morning hours of the following day and six days later was put to rest. In the low lights of the funeral parlor where the casket lay, a heady floral scent of lilies and carnations permeated the air. Carl Kirshka and his wife, along with Chrissy, stood by Libby's closed casket amid a backdrop of flower arrangements. Mourners queued up to shake the family's hands, exchange small talk, and embrace them with heart-felt hugs. A sob emanated from somewhere while a low murmur of hushed voices filtered through the room.

The line of people who came to pay their respects to the family wound around the perimeter of the viewing room with the tail ending up in the lobby. Alongside her mother, Chrissy stood closest to her sister's casket and nodded absently at each mourner as they extended sympathy to her and her family.

At the gravesite, an unseasonably cold wind tore through the nearby trees. It was the kind of rawness that made its way unbidden even through layers of clothing. An uninvited mourner. November air held no sentiment. High above, the sun shone more like a sickly version of itself, casting pale light through a scrim of clouds.

Chrissy stood stoically with her parents and the other mourners under the wind-whipped canopy at the gravesite as low clouds morphed from gray to dark sapphire. Peoples' eyes shone glassy as they stood like reverent statues bracing the cold as well as their emotions the best way they could. Except Chrissy's eyes were bone dry. She tried to force tears to come but nothing came. She wanted to mirror the same demeanor as the others around her who cried. Her emotions were normally as fragile as icicles that clung to the distant pines of winter, though not today. Right now, they mirrored the cold, dry November wind.

Chapter Nineteen

"There hasn't been a day in my life that I haven't thought about my little sister and what I did or didn't do to save her that day. I hated myself for it." Christine looked up at John, her eyes beseeching. "And I still do." She cast her eyes back down. "You must hate me, too. I wouldn't blame you."

John didn't speak at first. The impact of her story hit like a bomb exploded. He let the weight of her words and the moment settle before speaking. Then he reached across the table for her hand. "I feel your grief, Chris, and, of course, I don't hate you. That's silly. I can't even imagine going to that extreme. I've always been fond of you." He smiled. "Well, more than fond." He squeezed her hand. "That's why I told your father about the internship at the company, hoping you'd take it when you graduated."

"You gave me a great opportunity, but . . . "

"But what? You're Christine Kirsh of MNN news. You're an on-air talent in the fifth largest market in America."

"Pfftt . . . no. Changing my name and giving me a platform doesn't change who I am. I will always be Chrissy Kirshka, the loser daughter. The shadow daughter who longed for her parent's approval but it rarely, if ever, came. No, I'm nothing special and never will be."

John gripped her hand. "How could you even say that?"

"I really didn't want her dead," she explained. "But I felt this rush come over me—an adrenaline rush. It all happened so fast that I . . . I don't really remember every detail. But what I do remember is that I saw her fall into the water. It was like slow motion, and then I heard the crack of her skull on the rocks. I went into shock and felt like I was passing out."

"Do you think the shock possibly prevented you from jumping in to save her?"

"I don't know, John."

"Chris, I don't really think you were culpable in your sister's death. Quite the contrary. I think you were incapacitated, totally in shock. Do you really think you're capable of committing such a crime?"

"I think there's something wrong with me. And I've never gotten over it, frankly. Her death haunts me all the time."

"Chris, please."

She shook her head. "No, there's something seriously wrong. I mean, I could really *hate* her at times. I was alright for a while, had buried my feelings, I guess. But then I got a call from my Aunt Muriel not long ago, and the conversation turned to Libby."

John studied her. He could tell she was struggling and deeply troubled. He just didn't know how serious it had become. Had it been jealousy that turned into something evil? He didn't want to think she could be capable of murder, but the heart is desperately wicked, this he knew.

John lent a reassuring smile, though it didn't seem to affect her at all. Normally, she'd melt into a puddle, particularly if he'd given her a wink along with a smile. Not today. John knew she was grateful for her job and for their relationship that had evolved over the past year despite the age difference. *Had her heart hardened?* John's heart, in turn, softened all the more for her. The fated news of her sister's story coming out must have resurrected the dreaded feelings that she'd long buried. Now, her past had come back to bite her a second time.

"I'm so sorry for the trouble I've caused you."

"What are you talking about?"

Christine pursed her lips and shrugged. "Everything, just everything."

"Chris, I'm not following."

"John, this story and your son's involvement back then . . . now you know that he really didn't have much—if anything—to do with it."

"He *did*, Chris. He was there . . . because of the marijuana. If no one else knows of that fact, I do. It's his own damn fault. Meanwhile, the consequences of his actions are what stirred this problem—for all of us, and now we're living this whole damned saga all over again."

"No, we're not," she said, her eyes blazing. "I'll see to that."

"How?"

"I'll make sure that story doesn't go to print. It's the least I can do for you."

"Chris, I appreciate your help, but how are you going to do that?"

"I've gotta go now, John." She picked up her handbag and raincoat and scooted out of the booth.

"Where are you going?" John's voice rose. "Chris!"

Christine didn't answer nor turn back to look at him. She resolutely strode out the door of the restaurant into the night.

Chapter Twenty

"So, how's the story coming?"

"Not sure, really. I'd hoped for a bite from someone by now."

Craig's brows crinkled. "Didn't they reply?"

"I'm still waiting."

"Do they know you're a professional writer?"

Marly shrugged.

"Marly, you've fought for the little girl. Now, you've gotta fight for your story, too."

"You sound like me."

"Don't give up."

"You know me."

"Actually, I'm proud of you for not letting anything stop you."

"Funny, you should say that."

"What?"

"Not letting anything stop me. Those were the words I got in a blind e-mail the other day."

"Who'd send you a blind e-mail?"

"If I knew, it wouldn't be blind, goof."

"What did it say, exactly?"

"I deleted it."

"I would have kept it."

"I thought about it, but it just seemed too weird. I remember it said something like, *you'd better stop right now. Just stop. Your plans won't work out . . . something like that.*"

"Obviously, someone doesn't like what you're doing."

"But what am I doing that's so wrong? It's a story for Pete's sake. A story that's already been exposed to the public. No great shakes to bring it alive again. Should I report this to anyone?"

"Check with Microsoft. I'm sure they have a logistics department. Maybe they can locate the computer through an IP address, unless the person used an encrypted email or an anonymous email service. Then you're out of luck."

"Sounds like a lot of hassle. I'm not going to bother unless it happens again. So frustrating. By the way, did you hear about Ethan?"

"What about him?"

"Dee told me that he has some kind of cancer."

"Geez. He never mentioned anything to me."

"She said she found the doctor's note he apparently threw away. I guess he was keeping it from her. Can you imagine?"

"What stage?"

"Don't know."

"Sucks."

"I'd like to help cheer her up somehow, maybe take her shopping or something. She hasn't been answering my calls. Not sure what that's about. So, I think I'll drive over to her house and check in on her."

****

"John?" Tony, the lead traffic operations producer at MNN stood at John Strauss's office door. "Got a sec?"

John glanced up from his desk. "Hey, Tony. How was your weekend?"

"Decent."

"Catch anything?"

"A couple of bass and just missed getting a swordfish."

John grinned. "Next time."

"Yeah . . . hey, heads up . . . just wanted you to know Christine's not here."

"She's not?"

"She's not in her studio. The lights are still off."

"That's odd."

"I know. She's usually here by now, especially on Mondays. And her shift starts soon." He glanced at his watch. "It's almost four o'clock."

"Did you try calling her?"

"Not yet. Just thought you should know."

"I'll call her." John picked up the phone. "In case she's running late due to car trouble or something, is anyone able to fill in?"

"No worries, I'll ask Emily to cover for her."

"Thanks, Tony. Appreciate it." John gave him a thumbs up sign and then pressed the speed-dial number for Christine. He waited on the line. When her voicemail kicked in, he hung up and tried again. Still no answer. *This isn't good.*

John went down the hall to the main studio and stopped to observe the efficient hum of a typical day in the Broadcast Operations department. A dozen closed-circuit monitor screens displayed strategic camera angles along most all of the major roadways throughout Philadelphia and southern New Jersey. Several scanners picked up police reports and call outs, while Tony communicated on the two-way radio. From what it sounded like, the pilot noticed something as he flew over Valley Forge Park. Police and fire rescue teams were being dispatched.

"Ten-four," Tony replied to the pilot. Then he moved to one of the suburban cameras and began adjusting the viewfinder. He panned the camera and paused to focus on some flashing lights. From the chatter on the scanners, there was some kind of disturbance at the park.

John stepped closer to the monitor as Tony adjusted the lens. "Can you see anything?"

"Fire and rescue approaching the scene now, sir."

"What happened?" one of the sales reps from Marketing commented as she strolled through the Ops area.

Others gathered around the monitor to take a look at the flashing lights, trying to make sense of the seriousness of the scene.

"Where's this? What are we looking at?" another co-worker chimed in.

Tony explained the announcement that recently came in on the scanner alerting to a possible *1056-A* at Valley Forge Park. "Not seeing much right now." He panned up to and across the covered bridge toward the trees by the river.

"Oh, wait. Is that something there?" one of the anchors asked.

Others stepped out of their studios and joined those who'd gathered around to see what the commotion was all about.

"Not sure." Tony continued panning the camera. "I'm not seeing anything yet. Could be a false alarm."

John checked the time, now well past the start of the afternoon shift. He walked out of Ops and down the hall to the row of studio anchor booths. At the end of the row sat Studio D where Christine did her on-air reporting. The booth was empty. No lights on. Hopefully, Emily was doing Christine's reports from her own studio. For the past year, Christine had always been on time for work. Never late or absent. A star employee. Her pleasant on-air voice had even garnered a nomination for a broadcasting award by her peers. This wasn't like her.

John peered inside her studio through the glass door. From what he could see, everything appeared neat and organized. Not a pen or pencil out of place, the way she always left things. He got a strange feeling in the pit of his stomach when he spotted a piece of paper lying on the keyboard next to her computer.

John stepped inside and turned on the lights. While seated at her console, he examined the paper. It was a sheet of legal pad yellow paper with a few words written in black ink that had been scribbled out. It was probably something to be tossed that never made it to the trash, most likely the beginning notes of an assignment or a report. As he turned to leave, he caught a glimpse of the trash can next to her desk. Discarded cups and balled up paper filled most of it. Sitting near the top was another piece of yellow paper. He stared at the handwriting. It was definitely hers. On the first line she'd written the name *John*.

Chapter Twenty-one

THROUGHOUT THE DAY, MARLY'S thoughts kept circling back to Dee. Her heart tore for her friend's situation and the news of Dee's long-time boyfriend's cancer scare. Add to that the stress from working for her tyrant of a boss, the situation could put just about anyone into a funk, even as much as not feeling up to answering Marly's calls.

Marly pulled up to Dee's house late in the afternoon. Apparently, Dee was working at home since her car sat in its usual spot. That was one of the benefits to her job, especially since her boss kept her working at all hours. *He thinks he's a doctor*, she once quipped. *Or a god*.

As Marly walked along the sidewalk leading to Dee's house, she noticed a familiar face. There stood one of her former co-workers with his dog.

"Hey, Jason," she called out with a wave.

He glanced up. "Marly!"

"This is wild. I didn't know you lived around here."

"Yeah, about a year now. Nice to see you."

"Same here." She pointed to Dee's unit. "I'm here to visit a friend."

He nodded as his dog yanked on the leash. "Calm down, Pepper," he said to the furry canine that presented like a cross between a terrier and a blood hound.

Marly grinned at the struggle the dog gave him. "You've got a mission there, I see."

"Yeah, for sure."

"Well, good to see you."

"Yeah, good to see you, too."

"I miss you guys. Please send my best to everyone."

"Will do," he called back.

Marly ran up the steps to Dee's place and pressed the buzzer.

"Hey, there," Dee said, opening the door. "What brings you out this way?"

"Well, since you aren't answering your phone, lately,"—she put a hand on her hip—"I thought I'd come calling. I was worried."

"Oh, crap, I *did* get your message." Her hand flew to her forehead. "Sorry, Mar, I'm just so swamped—"

"Hey, I can come back—"

"No, no, it's fine,"—she gestured with her hand—"please, come in."

****

Dee and Marly hung out for a while, sharing the latest news of interest with each other just like old times. Friends since college, they could talk about the most intimate of details without any qualms. Marly tried to get Dee to laugh as much as possible, hoping to lift her sagging spirits. The topic eventually turned to Ethan.

"What's going on with his cancer . . . has he started treatments?"

"He's so tight lipped about it. I mean, all I want to do is be there for him, and he seems just so distant and withdrawn."

"He doesn't want to talk about it?"

"No, not in the least. It's weird, frankly."

"Maybe he's too frightened to talk about it. Most guys just like to bury their feelings, you know that."

Dee shook her head. "I don't know. I really don't."

"Well, all you can do is pray for him."

"I've been."

"Craig and I, too."

"Thanks."

Marly checked the time. "You look like you need to eat. Wanna head to the mall? We can get some dinner and then window shop. Or go for a hike up in Valley Forge? Oh, man, remember the last time we were shopping, and that little velvet purse with the gemstones on it dropped at my feet the second we left the store?"

Dee's lips curled up. "How could I forget?"

"It was somehow clinging to my coat. I still can't figure that one out. I didn't know if you believed me or not when I swore I didn't steal it."

"I believed you . . . eventually." Dee chuckled. "Your face . . . it looked so—"

"Mortified?"

"Yes, mortified."

"Ah, good times. So, what d'ya say? Dinner's on me."

Dee shook her head. "Thanks, but . . . "

"C'mon, you gotta eat sometime."

"You know I'd love to, but Jen is coming over later, and my boss is on my back. I'm juggling a thousand things for him right now."

"Okay, not a problem. I understand, but I wish you'd let your work go for a bit. You need a break, woman."

"I know. Tell me about it."

Marly searched Dee's face—a pile of worry and fear in her eyes. They'd chatted about so many things, but Marly wondered whether there was something else on Dee's mind? Not wanting to push her, Marly, quietly resigned herself to the situation. If Dee wanted to broach the subject, she would. It was Dee's choice.

Marly glanced out the bay window. "Wow, that sunset is spectacular," she gushed as a black vehicle pulled into the cul-de-sac. *Must be Jen.* "Well, hey,"—Marly stood—"it was great catching up."

"Yeah, and I hope that pet project of yours about the little girl pans out."

"Me, too. I have a good feeling about it."

"Human interest pieces are always a winner."

"Hope so."

Dee followed Marly to the door and reached out to give her a hug. "Hey, nice of you to visit."

"That's what friends are for, Dee. And we'll be praying for Ethan."

"Thanks, Mar, Means a lot. I'm sure to Ethan, too."

As Marly stepped out the door, the blare of emergency vehicle sirens resounded in the near distance.

"Okay, be safe," Dee called with a wave.

Marly waved back. If Dee had said anything else, it was inaudible over the screeching sirens.

Chapter Twenty-two

JOHN REACHED DOWN TO pick up the paper. He recognized the familiar writing, the odd slant with flowery loops and circles instead of dots.

Dear John:

Thank you for all you've done for me. Please know how much I've appreciated you taking me under your wing. I've learned so much from you during my time at MNN, and I truly couldn't have asked for a sweeter boss. It's been the icing on the cake of our relationship. But the truth is, I can't find my place in life. There's nothing more that I can do for myself. I've been a mess for so long, it's catching up to me now.

I feel so guilty for what happened to my little sister, and I truly believe that I'm responsible for her death. Let it go on record as such. You shouldn't be held to blame nor your family. Your name needn't be dragged through the mud again.

I feel like I'm letting you down, but I need peace, and this is the only way I'll be able to get it. It's what's best.

Love always,
Chris

John stared at the words on the paper and wondered why she tossed the note away. If he hadn't seen it lying there, it would have gone unnoticed. Did she change her mind about whatever it was? *What's best? Chris, what are you talking about?* He was more confused now than ever.

A knock on the glass door startled him. Tony stood there with a pained look on his face.

"John, there's something you need to see."

"Is there a problem?"

"You could say that."

****

Several had gathered in Ops and stood huddled around the monitor where Tony slowly panned the camera to an area with a lot of trees.

"A *1056-A* is confirmed," he said.

"What's a *1056-A*?" the woman from Marketing inquired.

"Suicide attempt," Tony said, softly. He stopped panning and zoomed in on a figure. It appeared to be someone standing alone atop a mountain overlook.

"What are we looking at, Tony?" another asked.

Tony focused on the blonde-haired figure. Someone gasped, and John's stomach lurched at what he saw.

"Is that *Christine*?" The woman's hand flew to her mouth.

Most everyone remained silent as they watched the figure standing precariously on the edge of a precipice. A palpable hush filled the room. Only the intermittent chatter over a two-way radio, or the squawk of a police or fire department scanner punctuated the otherwise silence in the room.

Until then, only two people knew the gravity of the situation. Tony suspected what was possibly going on when he recognized the *1056-A* code that he picked up from the scanner. The other person was John.

John quickly put things together, including his last interaction with Christine, along with the letter he found. He swiftly bolted down the hall for the elevator. A sickening feeling landed in the pit of his stomach. *Please, Chris, no.*

Chapter Twenty-three

JOHN PRESSED THE BUTTON to call the elevator. It took forever to arrive, and once it did, everything moved in slow motion—the door opening . . . the ten-story descent . . . the doors parting open again at the lobby.

Like a sprinter in a 500-yard dash, he scrambled across the polished floor and flew out the revolving door. He hopped into his car, turned on the ignition and sped out of the parking lot.

Why, Chris? John's thoughts ran wild as he sped west on I-76. He'd recognized the place in Valley Forge Park where she stood high above on the mountain's overlook. Seeing her sent a pang to his heart. He hoped the person standing precariously on the mountainside wasn't Christine—just a look-a-like or a mirage, of sorts. What he wouldn't give to believe it was just some other woman and not her. He'd give anything. Though sadly, he recognized the location. It was her favorite spot. They'd been there together several times. She loved the majesty of the mountains and the sound of the trickling water below—always claiming the charged ions in settings like that were particularly soothing. It's why people gravitated to places with water and mountains every chance they got, she was fond of pointing out.

Rush hour traffic had always been a problem on I-76. John raced to pass the slower cars as he weaved and jockeyed for position. At the approach to the curve in the road that simultaneously rose in elevation, both lanes of traffic slowed as in a synchronized dance with all of the vehicles evenly pacing one another. Any other day, this felt calming to him, almost magical with everyone together going the same speed. Today, it was grueling. By his estimation, he could arrive at the park—barring any obstacles—at best between fifteen and twenty minutes, but that was on a good day. Today was not good. The queasy feeling in his stomach felt worse. Sweat pooled down his face and neck. His thoughts spun. *God, please keep her safe.*

****

Operator: 911, what's your emergency?

Caller: There's a woman on top of a cliff—on the ledge—screaming something.

Operator: Your location?

Caller: Valley Forge Park.

Operator: Where in the park?

Caller: Right off of the west entrance by Militia Line Drive.

Operator: You say she's on a cliff?

Caller: Yeah, right on the edge of a precipice. I think she might jump. Oh, God. Please help her.

Operator: Can you describe the person?

Caller: Blonde hair. About five feet tall, maybe. Thin. Around 25-30ish . . . it's hard to tell, actually.

Operator: Montgomery #20 dispatching you to Valley Forge Park. We have a report of a woman on a cliff near Militia Line Drive. . . . possible *1056-A*. Respond Code 3. Sending two units. Priority 1. Acknowledge.

Trooper Jenson: Copy that.

Trooper Morgan: Copy.

****

The vehicle traveling behind Marly had been there a while. Edging closer and then letting up a bit, the driver didn't seem like the patient type. *What is this person's problem?* There was no way she could go any faster in her Honda Civic and she wasn't about to speed up—not on this road. Something didn't seem right. The driver appeared satisfied to ride her tail. If this person were trying to be annoying, it was working.

Marly took a deep breath and released it slowly, hoping to calm herself. The rich bourbon scent of fall air coming through the partially open window could easily assuage her senses; though now, she barely noticed it. Her first inclination was to keep herself alive. Did the driver mean any harm? Was her imagination running away with her, or was this just a bad vibe? The driver's face remained obscured, though there was something odd about it. Whoever it was had an insane penchant for speed. She tried to think positively; after all, this was a single-lane road in each direction. There was bound to be someone else traveling through the park at the same time. She took another calming breath and tightly clutched the wheel while glancing in the rearview mirror again, hoping the car was gone. Its headlights were now on and glared like obnoxious eyes.

Tension drew into her neck and shoulders as she gripped the wheel. *Just hold on, Marly. Be patient. This person will get the chance to pass at some point.* The headlights behind her held a determination, almost mockingly, and reminded her of an old Stephen Spielberg movie when a crazy truck driver tailed the hero for miles on a lonely highway. It was all she could take when up ahead a rocky overhang and jutting tree limbs startled her as they stretched out across the roadway like sinister skeletal arms threatening to scoop up her car. *Lord, stay with me.* Marly's palms grew moist as she gripped the wheel. She steeled herself to get through the ride.

After a while, raindrops began tapping the windshield before a downpour hit. The rain pummeled loudly on the roof of the car, and she quickly flipped on the windshield wipers, but they didn't help much to clear the water that fell no less forceful than a water-fall. Hopefully, with the rain now beating down, the driver tailing behind would have the common sense to ease up on the speed.

A moment later, in her peripheral vision, she noticed the presence of something to her left. *Was the car finally passing?* The rain clouded things to the point where she wasn't sure, but it lent a bit of relief if it was, indeed, the car that had been tailing her.

Finally, yes, something passed on the left. *Thank God!* Even better, she was almost to the main road that led back home in just another half-mile or so. A sense of peace slowly eased the tension in her back and neck. She loosened her tight grip on the wheel and could finally breathe.

Boom!

No sooner did she begin to relax than a sudden jolt sent her heart racing all over again. The vehicle traveling directly behind smacked into her back end, sending the car lurching forward. Despite her focus and careful steering, she lost control. The tires were now taking her off the road, veering onto its own path. The rumble of uneven terrain caused the car to shake. Seized with panic, the dire situation sent her spiraling as the car bounced over rocks and above ground tree roots while she stomped her foot hard on the brakes. *Stop! Oh, God, no!* Jamming the brake pedal repeatedly did nothing to halt the momentum of the car now heading straight for the riverbank. As the car careened to-ward the water, her heart pounded out of her chest. Adrenaline surged through her body. An instant later, the car banged into a tree and then rebounded onto the embankment.

Perched at the edge of the water on top of a huge bolder nestled in the ridge, the car slowly tipped downward, rocking slightly before it slowly nosed into the water. Water rose up onto the car hood. Moments later, the car dipped lower into the dark brown river.

Chapter Twenty-four

"CONFIRM LOCATION," EMT JIM PARKER called out over the two-way.

"Valley Forge Park . . . the river adjacent to Militia Line."

"Copy that."

"Jimmy, hold up, I can't find my phone," said his partner, Al, as he searched his locker. "Ah, here it is. Never mind, we're good."

"Okay, let's roll."

Jim raced through the park. His body thrummed with anticipation. Never knowing what to expect on any given EMS assignment was the best job in the world as far as he was concerned. If he couldn't be a doctor, this was the next best thing. With each call, he had one more chance to help save a fellow human's life.

Spotting the flashing lights of the police and fire rescue squads at the scene, his pulse ticked up. He loved his work, and the natural high it gave him was only a bonus. He turned off the road as close to the river as possible and parked directly behind a fire truck.

Jim unfastened his seatbelt. "Looks bad."

"Holy mother, looks like it's almost totally submerged," Al replied. "Or maybe, it's just the angle."

Jim shook his head and opened the door. "Gonna take a miracle."

Jim and Al introduced themselves to the responders from the local marine unit as a burly man hoisted a cable from the truck.

Two others were there with hip waders and began to descend into the river, while two more looked on.

"River energy flow is high. We'll need to work quickly," one of the responders said. "Seems we're in a decent spot here—for now." The murky brown water slushed around the two front tires of Marly's car and splashed up onto the hood.

"Think it's best we make a wedge," the burly man advised. "Check how many occupants."

"I'm on it," called out another from the marine unit, who stepped into the muddy bank and waded to the front of the car. He peered inside the partially open window and saw Marly—pale and with closed eyes. "One victim inside. Female. Don't know if she's responsive," he shouted. He struggled to reach inside to find a way to check her pulse. She was alive but had lacerations on her forehead. "A lot of blood here," he yelled.

"Do we need to bring the boat in?" asked another marine officer.

"Water level isn't high enough, wading is fine. Hey, Ethan, how about being third man in for the wedge . . . can ya handle it?"

"Of course, I'm on it." Ethan grabbed a set of PPE from the truck and began to suit up.

"Need a line?"

"No, she isn't responsive," the man in the water shouted.

"No tow line then. Get her a regulator—fast. And we'll use the winch cable."

"Securing it now."

"Got the shackles?"

"Right here."

"Better anchor them tight. Good thing she's wedged to the rock, otherwise this thing's a goner."

"Sir, the water level is rising," second marine officer Rosario shouted. "The eddy is downstream. We gotta work fast or we'll be in trouble should this car shift any more. It could fall on top of us."

"Got it. No worries. Already got a shackle on. We'll be fine. Everything's secured. You worry too much, Rosario."

"Just sayin' it's rising." He raised his arms in frustration. "Don't tell me I didn't warn you."

As two of the officers began to secure the shackles onto the rear tire rims, a sudden shift of the car tore away the hold.

Shouting an expletive, the lead officer shook his head and called out. "Oh, for crying out loud. No, no, hold up. The car is shifting. Stop!"

"Damn it, I can't control it. We're going farther in. Ethan, hold up."

*****

Valley Forge Park swiftly turned into chaos in a matter of minutes. With two serious situations, local police and rescue teams had their hands full and desperately needed back-up assistance. While one emergency team struggled with the car threatening to fall into the river, another crew stood by to talk a woman safely off the mountain where she stood in a precarious position overlooking the river. Neighboring jurisdictions in the tri-county area were dispatched to help as manpower was now at a premium.

The men involved with securing the car worked feverishly while others just paced. Ethan, now restless himself, walked over to the edge of the river. He looked over at the woman inside the partially submerged vehicle. When he studied the situation further, his heart kicked up a notch as he recognized her. *Marly?* The woman behind the wheel whose life was in danger was his friend.

"I'm going in," Ethan shouted.

"No, the eddy is too strong, it'll be dangerous."

"I'll be fine."

"Wait. You'll be gambling with her life and yours."

"We're in the mud, hold on." The first officer shook his head. "This isn't good."

"Damn right, it's not good. The water level is rising!"

"Told you." Rosario flung his hands up.

"Just wait it out. Let the current go. Don't fight it, man!"

As the water level rose, the hood of the car was now completely covered and rising fast onto the windshield. By all accounts the level could rise above the side windows in another minute. At that point, they'd have to break the glass to get Marly out. Ethan's pulse raced. He had to save this woman.

Chapter Twenty-five

ANOTHER HORRIFIC SCREAM CUT through the canyon. At this point, the woman's screams eventually drew the attention of park dwellers down by the river. By now, a local news van was on the scene with a cameraman filming the blonde-haired woman high above them.

Officer Jenson stared up at the woman. "What is she saying?"

His partner shook his head. "She's either crazy or just wants attention."

"You don't think she'll jump?"

"Oh, for sure that's a possibility."

Officer Jenson hurried over to the squad car and retrieved a bullhorn. Mentally, he went over the points he'd learned in dealing with suicide prevention: listen, empathize, build rapport. There was more, but it was all he could remember at the moment. Moving as close to the river's edge as possible to get a clearer view of the woman, he called out to her.

"I'm Officer Rod Jenson. Do you need help, ma'am?" There was no reply. "We're here to help you." He tried to show as much kindness as he could so as not to startle or disturb her, asking her name and other innocuous questions to distract her. Still, not a word came from the woman.

"Should we go up?" Officer Morgan asked.

"You mean sneak up behind her?"

"Yeah, and throw a catch-net."

"Not a bad idea. There's one in the trunk or should be. Lemme check." Minutes later, he came back holding the net. "Got it."

"Now, how to get up there is the bigger question."

"We approach from behind."

"Do you know the trails?"

"They should be marked. Let's go."

"No, I'll go. You stay here to distract her."

Just before Officer Morgan left, John, totally out of breath, stumbled up to the scene and approached the officers.

"Where is she?" he asked, breathing heavily. He rubbed his chest as though in pain.

The officers turned to appraise him. Officer Jenson asked, "You are?"

"My name's John Strauss." He huffed, breathlessly, and looked up, searching for Christine. "She's up there, somewhere . . . "—he pointed—"she works for me. Her name is Christine. Christine Kirsh." He held his chest as though about to pass out.

The officers exchanged glances. "Christine Kirsh," Officer Jenson repeated. Name's familiar."

"Christine Kirsh . . . from the news?" Officer Morgan added.

John nodded.

"You don't look well. Are you alright?" Officer Jenson asked.

John frowned and shook his head. "No, I'm not good. Not at all. I'm a mess, but . . . "—he looked up to see if he could spot Christine—"we've got to get her down."

Chapter Twenty-six

ETHAN ASSESSED THE SITUATION, wishing the horror before him wasn't real and only a nightmare. He'd had better, for sure. Ones where his heart didn't race out of control or fear rise up to consume him, where at any given moment the scene could swiftly change. Unfortunately, this wasn't imagery in his subconscious; this was his reality. Also, it was his chance to be the hero in this story. If anyone were going to save Marly, it would be him. He had more than one reason to risk his life for this woman.

In the midst of the rushing river, he eyed an odd patch of swirling water forming a whirlpool effect about a yard or so in front of the car. He'd seen documentaries about them but couldn't recall whether it involved sharks or something else. It reminded him of a swirling drain, but since this was a fairly shallow river as far as he knew, he dismissed it. How much danger could a whirlpool cause? Obviously, it wasn't from a low head dam where a submerged hydraulic jump could form, producing an upstream current that would inversely pull a person under the water. No, he'd be fine. Also, the rear tires had been secured, so the car wasn't going anywhere. At least as long as the cable didn't slip again. It was now or never. He braced himself for the plunge and jumped feet first into the cold river.

Ethan fought the onslaught of water that rose and churned. He'd battled intense fires and had fended off feral dogs and other wild animals in his job over the years, but dealing with the incessant rush of powerful water that usurped his strength, he knew he was no match for it. Still, he fought to squelch his fear. He needed to save Marly. In that moment, everything crystallized, and he realized why. His heart leapt inside his chest. Feelings that he'd squelched over the years came pouring out. They were as strong as the waves that threatened to outdo him. In the moment, he said a silent prayer. Only God's strength could handle this situation. *Lord, I need her. Please save her.*

A wave of water flew up and drenched his face. He choked and coughed the water out. The currents lapped over and over, mockingly, as the threat of his drowning hovered just beyond the brink. *God, please help me.* He knew God was with him as he searched through his soaked pocket for the hammer to break the window. Moments later, he saw something that defied all odds: The nose of the car began to slowly drop downward. He cursed and yelled back to the rescuers on the bank, "It's moving, it's moving . . . what the hell, secure it already, damn it. This isn't good!"

Up on the bank, the lead officer from the marine unit yelled back something inaudible. The man's hands flew up in frustration, and two others joined him at the back of the car to deal with the cable malfunction. Meanwhile, Ethan barely had anything to hold onto and was fearful for his own life. He reached out for the side of the car, but his hand kept slipping. Marly's window was partially open, thankfully. He still needed to break it totally to get her out, but first he had to find the hammer to smash the glass. He was so wired that he couldn't remember in which pocket he'd placed it.

"Crap, where is it?" His fingers probed inside the tight pocket space. Cold river water pooled at the base of his neck and poured down his back. *No, I'm not giving up.* He continued taking in as much air as he could before another current of water could knock him off course. He figured he had at least sixty to ninety seconds to work with and fought to ignore the chilling cold that numbed his body.

His mind raced while recalling his training for just such an incident. *First step, don't panic.* He took another large breath before more water rose. All the while he struggled to find the hammer.

85

He jammed his hand into the other pocket until the tip of his finger brushed up against something hard. *Yes.* Yanking the hammer from his soaked pocket, he engaged the spring-loaded feature and hoped the glass window was tempered and not laminated. The latter wouldn't budge even with a deluxe model. On top of everything else, a sudden downpour of rain clouded his vision. He poised his arm to jab the window, hoping the glass would not get into her eyes nor his should it fracture. He aimed and swung hard—once, twice, and by the third time, the window shattered. Some of the glass struck his face, but he ignored it.

Ethan grabbed Marly by the waist of her jeans and yanked her up and out of the car. Another rescuer managed to get close enough to the edge of the bank to extend a long pole to help guide them safely out. Wrapping her in a headlock he'd learned in water safety class, he was able to pull her along while holding onto the pole.

"They're pulling her out now," the second responder called out and rushed down the embankment. "Stay with us ma'am. Yo, Rosario, grab a blanket for her." Meanwhile two others from the marine unit followed him and helped Ethan carry her to the top of the bank.

"Is she breathing?" Jim asked as he rushed to assist.

No one knew, so Jim stretched her out and immediately performed two rescue breaths. She then began to cough. They quickly turned her onto her side. Water spewed out while Ethan and another from the squad held her.

"Let it all out," Ethan said as he slapped her upper back.

Jim reached for her arm. "Can you tell me your name?" He checked her pulse. White as chalk and shivering, Marly bore signs of hypothermia. "She'll need to get to the hospital," he told one of the officers.

"Mar," she began. "Name's Marly," she managed to choke out.

Ethan bent down and wrapped his arms around her. "Marly, you're gonna be alright, I promise." He held her tightly, hoping she could feel the warmth of his body pressing into hers. She replied with a moan. Her eyes remained closed.

As Jim and the others from the marine unit kept an eye on her, the sound of a loud scream from high above them pierced the early evening air.

Chapter Twenty-seven

DEE SETTLED HERSELF ON the sofa and poured a glass of wine. Drained from staring at her computer all day, she closed her eyes and put her feet up on the coffee table in an effort to relax. While sipping her wine, she reached for the remote and turned on the TV. She flipped through the stations. Stopping at a *Breaking News* headline, flashing lights on the screen pulled her in. She stared in disbelief. Her relaxed state shifted to wide-eyed alertness at seeing a familiar red car being hauled out of the river.

"Oh my god, what?" she cried aloud. "Is that . . . ?" *Could it be?*

Dee jumped up and raced to pick up her phone lying on kitchen table and pressed the speed dial for Marly. No answer. She tried again. Then she texted Craig.

Dee: Craig, is Marly home? I'm watching the news, and it looks like her car went into the river or something. Tell me I'm seeing things. Please advise asap, thanks.

Craig: Just got a call from the hospital. She's at Bryn Mawr.

Chapter Twenty-eight

CRAIG DARTED FROM LANE to lane on Montgomery Avenue as he sped to the hospital. With his heart in his throat, he pressed his foot to the accelerator as fast as he could safely drive through town, cursing every slow car or lane restriction due to construction projects along the way. When he finally reached the hospital, Marly was still in the emergency room.

"I'm looking for my wife," Craig said to a passing nurse.

"Her name?"

"Marly Maines."

"Yes, okay. She's in bed seven, right around the corner over here, sir."

Craig followed the nurse, who parted the curtain of the unit where Marly laid.

"We have her on a hemodialysis machine to rewarm her blood and circulate it back into her body. In a few minutes, we'll check her temperature again." The nurse adjusted the thick blanket on the bed where Marly laid like an Eskimo wrapped in a cocoon. "Then she can have warm fluids administered through IV," the nurse stated.

"What's the mask for?" Craig asked with a frown.

"Oxygen. She'll need it for a while."

Craig stared in disbelief at the sight of his wife. Her forehead lacerations were bandaged, and he was afraid to ask if anything else had been damaged. Near tears, he sat at the foot of her bed holding himself together as best as he could. Over the next hour, he sat and waited for his wife to open her eyes. She'd be recovering soon, the nurse and attending physician both agreed. If only they could be sure of it. Anything is possible, Craig knew. Only time would tell.

Chapter Twenty-nine

THE NEXT DAY . . .

Marly opened her eyes and saw Dee standing at the foot of the bed.

"Hey, there. How are you feeling?"

"Not sure if I've had enough drama."

"I see your sarcasm is still alive and well."

"What 'cha got there?"

Dee held up a vase of colorful balloons attached to a bouquet of flowers. "I know how much you love them."

"Sweet of you."

"You want them here?" Dee set it on the table. "Or over there?" She pointed to the windowsill.

"Doesn't matter."

"As long as you can see them. Like you've always told me: *Viewing flowers helps the healing process.*"

"It's true. I really believe it. And they don't suck up the oxygen in the room." Marly chuckled at recalling what someone said once when she'd brought flowers to the nursing home. "Oy. Hope I don't get that kind of crazy when I get old."

"Pretty flowers," a perky nurse announced as she strode in with a smile. "So, how are you Ms. Maines?"

"Just a little tired is all."

"Doctor been in yet?"

"Not yet. But I'm feeling much better."

"Good to hear. Doctor wants to check on your potassium level and also the EKG results, I believe that's what's in order. But if everything checks out—"

"I can go home?" Marly cut in.

"That's the plan," she said with a wink. "So, okay. In the meantime, I'm going to have someone bring you some soup and a hot beverage, if you're up for it?"

"Sure."

"Do you have a choice of what you'd prefer?"

"Hot tea would be fine, preferably green. And chicken soup would be great."

"You got it."

When the nurse left the room, Dee's eyes lit up. "Wow, that's service. Do they recognize you or something?"

"I'm sure it's SOP, especially for traumatic car crash victims."

"Still, I'm impressed.

"Me, too."

"So, tell me about that accident. When I saw what looked like your car on the news, I immediately texted Craig. How'd you end up in the river?"

"It was wild. Unbelievably insane. This driver behind me . . . who knows who it was. It was hard to tell, really. Anyway, at one point, I looked in my rearview mirror, and for a second, I could have sworn it was my old boss!"

"What? From MNN?"

"Yep, kind of looked like him."

"Oh, no!"

"Anyway, this person was tailing me through Valley Forge Park when I was on my way home from your house. Then after a couple of miles of kissing my bumper, the next thing I hear—and feel—is a *bang*."

"Oh, Marly, I can't even imagine. Was the person going to a fire or something?"

"Actually, there were fire trucks not far from where I got hit . . . flashing police lights and everything, but it's all such a blur now."

"Oh, wow, you poor thing. I'm sure it was awful."

"All I remember is my car getting jolted and then flying on its own right off the road and onto the creek bank. I totally lost control. Wasn't long before it just tipped into the river."

"You must've been so scared."

"Out of my mind. It was unreal. Then I hit my head, and I was unconscious for a bit."

"I'm so sorry, Mar. I can't believe this happened."

"It was crazy."

Just then an orderly came in wheeling a tray.

"Oh, here comes my meal." She sat up as he put the tray down on the bedside table. "Thank you, sir."

Marly took the lid off the soup and unwrapped the package of crackers. "Well, it was sweet of you to come, Dee. Thanks for making the trip."

"Sounds like you want to get rid of me."

"No way. But I don't think you want to hear me slurping my soup."

"Okay, you've got a point, but all the same, I should be going." She picked up her bag and slung it over her shoulder. "I'm sure you need to stay low-key for a while and get some rest. You've been through a major shock to your system. Just get well, okay?"

"I'll do my best."

"I'll catch up with you soon."

"It's a plan."

Chapter Thirty

Later that evening . . .

Covered in layers of bed clothing, Marly drifted off to sleep until something awakened her. She opened her eyes to find a tall person standing at the foot of the bed holding a vase of coral red roses and baby's breath. A smile spread across his face. As her eyes focused more clearly, her heart skipped.

"Ethan!"

"Hey, Sunshine."

"Are those for me?"

"Well, they're not for your nurse," Ethan said with a wink.

"The color is awesome."

He placed the roses next to the balloon bouquet.

"Dee was here earlier. She brought those flowers."

"And balloons?" He grinned. "How'd she ever know you love balloons?"

"Ha, right," Marly said at the private joke. "I guess my secret is out."

Ethan's eyes crinkled as he held a smile. His piercing eyes seemed to drink her in.

"So, how're y' feeling? You look much better than yesterday."

"How do you know what I looked like yesterday?"

"I was there."

"You were there?"

"You don't remember? You were in a pretty bad way yesterday."

"Yeah, the accident. How could I forget, but . . . "

"I pulled you out of the river, Mar."

His words found a beeline to her heart. The warmth surpassed anything a blanket could provide. Filled with both gratitude and unbelief, she didn't know quite what to say. *Thank you* wasn't enough.

"You saved my life?"

While standing across from her bed, Ethan's face grew red. He gave a brief shrug.

"And risked yours in doing it? I-I don't know how to thank you. I really don't."

"All in a day's work."

"Right." She grinned. "Like you get called for a rescue mission out on the river every day."

Ethan modestly looked away for a moment and then back up at her. His eyes sparkled when he smiled, something she noticed ever since they met years ago.

"I must have been unconscious for a while, right?"

"Yes, you were."

"I appreciate what you did for me, Ethan. Thank you from the bottom of my heart."

"Just get well. That'll be my thanks."

"I'll do my best. Hey, by the way, I heard about your medical issue. I was so sorry to hear about it. Dee told me."

Ethan blushed again.

In the shared silence, Marly immediately regretted bringing up the subject. By mentioning it, she may have opened a topic she wasn't sure he wanted to talk about. He rubbed both hands down his neck and let out a protracted sigh. She wondered what was going through his head. The weight of the moment pressed in. Cancer. What a heavy load to bear. Her sympathy went out to him and all who loved and cared about him.

Ethan locked eyes with hers. His stare was warm, but there was something else behind his gaze that she couldn't decipher. Normally, he was an open book, his feelings displayed on his sleeve, his body language usually speaking volumes. Though this time, she couldn't get a read.

"Let's not talk about that, okay?"

"Oh, sure. Absolutely. I'm sorry, but—"

"It's okay. *I'm* okay. Just know that everything is all right with me."

Marly felt confused; her head still felt a bit foggy. She wanted to believe he was healthy, and if he said he was okay, she believed him.

****

"Ms. Maines," Dr. Robertson said as he entered the room. He went to her bedside, briefly glancing at Ethan. "I have some good news for you. Your tests have shown positive results. Your EKG shows to be normal and your numbers are in good range."

Marley smiled. "That's great to hear."

"Indeed." He tapped his pen on the chart. "Now, you may feel a bit fuzzy headed for another day or two, but that's normal. Of course, your body may still remain a bit stiff, and your head lacerations will take time to heal. Otherwise, you're on your way back to health."

"So, I can go home soon?"

"Yes, you'll be discharged as soon as the paperwork is completed. Should be first thing in the morning. Oh, and I hope they find that hit-and-run driver who rammed your car."

"Thank you, doctor."

After the doctor left the room, something on the TV caught Marly's eye. A breaking news story chyron flashed on the screen.

"Oh, my god," she cried, reaching for the remote to power up the volume. "It's Christine Kirsh . . . from MNN. She's dead."

Chapter Thirty-one

"You say it was a hit-and-run?"

"Yes."

"When and where did it occur?"

"Last Monday evening at Valley Forge National Park."

"Has this been reported to the police?"

"Of course. It was a serious accident involving my wife, and they were on the scene."

"Any injuries?"

"Yes, she was hospitalized overnight after she lost consciousness. Lacerations and a bruised rib. She's home now."

"Who are you talking to?" Marly stage whispered to Craig as she came into the room.

He cupped the phone. "The insurance guy."

He continued the conversation and answered the rest of the agent's questions.

"Okay, Mr. Maines, I'll submit this and we'll be in touch."

"Great, thanks." Craig hung up the phone and joined her on the sofa. "The insurance company has the accident on record now. Hopefully, we'll get something back."

"I loved my little Honda," Marly said. "So dependable."

"We'll get you another one." He put his arms around her, and she snuggled herself into his chest.

"I'm so sorry," she breathed into his ear.

"You're sorry? *I'm* sorry. Babe, you were almost killed. For Pete's sake, what do you have to be sorry about?"

"The car. We're out a car now."

"Better than being out a wife. I'd love to know who that jerk was who clipped you. Like why were they going so fast to slam into you like that?"

"I was just thinking . . . "

"What?"

"It's weird, but when I looked in my rearview mirror a couple of times, I could have sworn it was my old boss in the car behind me."

"That's crazy. What color was the car?"

"I'm pretty sure it was silver. Or gray."

"What's he drive?"

"A Jag."

"Was there a hood ornament? Jaguars have them."

"I was too nervous to notice anything like that."

"Hmmm . . . "

"What are you thinking?"

"I'm thinking the police should know about this."

"They already know it was a hit-and-run, right?"

"Yes, but I mean the stuff you just mentioned—about your boss. When you were in the emergency room, one of the officers came to talk to you, but you weren't in the best of shape. They said they would come back. Did anyone come back later to see you?"

"No policeman, only Dee and Ethan stopped by."

Craig got up off the couch.

"Where are you going?"

"Going to the police."

"But the police report is already in."

"They don't know all the details, Mar. For instance, what you just told me about seeing your boss on the road. That's important for them to know."

"Okay, then I'm going with you."

****

Marly's nerves tightened as she and Craig ascended the steps to the police station. She hadn't done anything wrong and her conscience was clear, not even a parking ticket in as long as she could recall. Still, her nerves danced. She was glad Craig was there to do the talking.

"Here to speak with Corporal Lindstrom," Craig spoke into the speaker in the security window at the front desk. "We're Craig and Marly Maines."

"Please have a seat. He'll be with you shortly."

Chapter Thirty-two

"I'M A WHAT?" CRIED John to the police officer who showed up at his office. "Did you say, *a suspect*?"

"Not saying you're guilty, sir. Just need to place a hold on your vehicle while the Vehicle Crimes detective deals with it."

"What crime?"

"A car was hit in Valley Forge Park last Monday early evening matching your car's description."

"Who's car?"

"Belongs to Marly Maines."

"Marly Maines? But I didn't have an accident last Monday."

"Were you driving through the park at the time of the incident?"

"Monday? Well . . . I guess, yeah, I was." John's thoughts went back to the scene while racing to find Christine. "I was en route to a situation at the park—a very serious one involving one of my employees, Christine Kirsh. You may be familiar with what happened last Monday evening."

"The jumper? The lady who jumped off the mountain. That who you're talking about?"

"Yes."

"She worked for you?"

"Yes, she was a reporter."

The officer shook his head. "That's too bad."

"You don't know the half of it."

"I'm really sorry."

"Yeah, so am I. Hey, listen. Am I under arrest or something? Do I need to get my lawyer involved here?"

"You can answer any or all questions you want to, but please keep in mind that anything you say can be—"

"Yeah, yeah, I know the drill. Listen, this is nuts. I didn't have an accident. I didn't cause an accident. I'm innocent here."

"Okay, sir, it's your call, but I'd advise you to get in touch with your lawyer. I'll have to ask you to come down to the station first thing in the morning."

John's thoughts swirled after the police officer left. The shock of the imposing presence standing boldly in his office sent his blood pressure into overdrive. The weight of the world pressed in on his shoulders. Confused, broken . . . his heart couldn't bear much more grief. The death of Christine and the way she died by suicide was grievous enough. Now, the police suspected him of a hit-and-run accident involving a former employee? He imagined how the negative publicity would impact him as well as the company. Not to mention the Halloween story with the potential to defame his name all over again; it now paled in comparison to the current situation. Bad things come in threes, the superstitious always said. He dropped his head into his hands. This couldn't be happening.

The horrendous scream that reverberated through Valley Forge Park still echoed in his head. The evening Christine ended her life by jumping from a mountain precipice into the river below cut deep. *Sweet Christine.* He'd always been fond of her and suspected she was the fragile type, even as a young teenager when she babysat for his family. Quiet, sullen, her emotions simmered just below the surface, always in check as though she were afraid to be herself. Somehow, that was her charm—at least to him. Giving her the internship the summer before she graduated *cum laude* with a B.A. in Journalism from Bryn Mawr College lit her up. She excelled at public speaking and blossomed into her own. Though the baggage she carried with her was heavier than she'd let on—until it was too late.

There was nothing he could do about Christine's death. That was her own choice and doing. But this accident—a felony—he could control.

Chapter Thirty-three

MARLY STOOD STUNNED WHEN she answered the door. Standing there on the front stoop was her former boss, John Strauss.

"John? What do you want?"

"Please, Marly," he began. "I apologize for coming over unannounced. I hope this isn't an imposition for coming here."

"Um . . . well . . . "

"Actually, yes, it is," Craig retorted as he came up behind Marly. "Why aren't you locked up? Haven't you caused enough harm to this family?"

John put both hands up in a defensive posture. "No, no. Please, I need to speak with you," his voice urgent. "I need to speak with both of you. I've already talked to the police about it. Didn't they tell you?"

"No, they didn't," Craig snapped.

"Well, I'd like to, if you'll oblige me."

Craig started pushing the door closed, but Marly intervened. "Wait, Craig."

"Seriously, Marly?"

"Let's hear him out," she said under her breath. "Frankly, I'm curious."

****

John slapped his hands on his thighs. "So, that's everything. That's the whole gruesome story. Not only sad, it's just crazy."

"Wow, that's a lot to take in," Marly said as she and Craig exchanged glances.

"I'm sure all of this comes as a shock to you . . . it's been awful for all of us. I feel like I'm in my own alternate universe and every scene just doubles down on me."

Marly shook her head. "I can't believe what I'm hearing."

"God's honest truth, Marly. I'm probably as stunned as you are. I just wanted to get to Christine before it was too late. I'm so sorry if my urgency frightened you."

Marly waved her hand, dismissively. *I would have done the same thing.* "I can't believe Christine would take her life though. So, you think Christine felt guilt over her sister's death?"

John shrugged. "I'd like to believe that she was innocent of such a heinous crime, but in piecing the details together, what other conclusion is there?"

That maybe your son was involved? Marly's thoughts ran back to what Muriel had told her.

"There was a neighbor woman named Muriel," Marly began. "She mentioned your son and his pot smoking."

"Yes, I know Muriel. She's Christine's Great Aunt. A good woman but I never clicked with her. I know my son's history, but smoking pot and murdering a child are two different things. Really, I've been over this in my mind a thousand times, and it's just not true that my Steve would have anything to do with Libby's death."

"I wonder why Muriel claimed it was your son? She also implied that you had some sort of influence or something, and the police probably just looked the other way rather than bring you down."

"Oh, that's nonsense. If Steve were involved other than circumstantially, they'd be all over this case. They'd love to pull me down. But they've got nothing."

"But he was at the scene, right?"

"That's what I'm told. Steve was never clear about it—at least to me. But the cops got it all out of him and, apparently, whatever he told them was plausible. So, they never charged him. But Christine was at the scene, too. She told me so."

Craig waved his arm. "Okay, okay, that part of the story is one thing, but closer to home is my wife's situation. Someone ran her off the road. Are you saying that someone else hit Marly's car and not you?"

"I don't know. All I *do* know is that I didn't. I was speeding toward finding Christine. I felt like a madman and probably looked that way, too. But I would never intentionally hit someone's car."

Marly held her hand up. "John, I don't know what to say." She hung her head. After some silence, she looked up at him. "I'm so sorry for all of this. I can see how this has been a nightmare for you. And for what we were thinking"—Marly glanced at Craig— "we thought . . . well, we thought the worst. I felt like a character in a movie with a chase scene that I didn't sign up for."

"I'm sure you were scared out of your mind," he said. "In fact, I was, too. I felt the same way. I'm thinking this car behind me is gunning for something—or someone. That's why I turned off the road when I did."

"Could Christine have been the one who sent Marly those cease-and-desist emails?" Craig asked.

"Good question. Honestly, I don't know. Could have been. Were you guys close at all or more like rivals?"

"More like two rivals in a cut-throat business, I guess. But the emails were encrypted. Seems like the sender didn't want me to know their identity."

"Christine said she'd put a stop to getting the story out. She was so concerned for my reputation."

"Speaking of which, John," Marly began. "This really turns the Halloween story around. Seems like Christine's name should be included in the story if what you're saying is true."

"But then the onus is on Christine," he replied. He pursed his lips while shaking his head. "I'd hate to nail her for Libby's death."

"But if she's *culpable* . . . " Craig began. "If she's potentially culpable, that is, she may as well be allegedly guilty. I mean, not necessarily judged guilty but certainly under some kind of suspicion."

John shook his head. "But without due process, she's—"

"Due process?" Marly's voice rose. "Due process? She's dead. There is no due process."

"It's really only circumstantial evidence," John said.

Marly wondered if the information she'd gleaned from Muriel was accurate. *Did John's son have a hand in it, or was it Christine herself?*

Marly sighed. "Okay, we've been going around and around on this, I need a break." She got up and left the room.

Moments later, Craig spoke up. "Listen, John. We both know this story is incriminating, right?"

John's face reddened. "Sure is."

"In all fairness, I think it would be best if Marly wrote the story with both the Strauss name as well as Christine's. Casting aspersions on neither—just that they were nearby . . . that kind of thing. I think it would absolve your son in the court of public opinion if another party's name like Christine's was also mentioned, though without throwing her or anyone under the bus, of course."

"I don't know. I thought I'd gotten my son's name redacted according to someone who promised me it wouldn't appear in the papers back in the day, but as it turned out, it got printed anyway. So, whatever will be will be."

Marly came back into the room carrying a tray of ice water and three plastic cups.

"Honey, what if both names appear in your article—both Christine's and Steve Strauss? That way the Strauss name kind of just blends into the shadows of the story because, obviously, there was more than one person at the scene. And with each of them present, there's validation one to the other, kind of thing—"

"I'd prefer that no names appear," John broke in to say. "But it's not my call—not this time."

Marly frowned. "I've already submitted the story, but it doesn't seem to be getting any traction. It's weird."

"It'll get picked up," Craig said. "It's hot."

Marly's mind churned. "I'm not worried. It's just taking longer than I expected. I mean, what's the hold up?" She turned to John.

"And now we've got another issue to deal with, too. So, if it wasn't you who barreled into my car and knocking me off the road, then who did? And why haven't they come forward about it?"

"Looks like there's another case to put together," Craig said.

"Well, this one will be different," Marly replied. "This case is not going to sit unsolved for long. I'll be sure of it . . . whatever it takes."

Chapter Thirty-four

Session:

Dr. Kingsley: So, what's on your mind today?

Marly: Well, I've had a bit of an adventure since I last saw you.

Dr. Kinglsey: I'm listening.

Marly: I had a car accident, and a former colleague committed suicide.

Dr. Kingsley: Goodness, that's a lot of drama!

Marly: Yeah, tell me. There was a bit of a misunderstanding and, fortunately, that got cleared up, but there's still a major issue—a crime, in fact—that the police are working on. And I am, as well.

Dr. Kingsley: Of course, you're an investigative reporter.

Marly: I know, kind of strange that I'm investigating my own crime, right?"

Dr. Kingsley: What was the crime?

Marly: A hit-and-run accident.

Dr. Kingsley: Oh, you were involved in the hit-and-run? They hit you? Oh, that's nasty.

Marly: Yeah, it's been a bit much to figure out. First, I thought the driver was my boss. My *former* boss, that is.

Dr. Kingsley: Oh, no!

Marly: As it turns out, it wasn't him after all, thankfully.

Dr. Kingsley: So, it's a mystery still.

Marly: We're waiting for the police to identify the driver, if they can.

Dr. Kingsley: This must be so frustrating for you.

Marly: I'm wondering how someone could be so jaded that they wouldn't stop to help. After all, they were the one to bump into my car. Their car had to have been damaged, too, right? Seems only logical that they would want to . . . I don't know . . . help?"

Dr. Kingsley: People don't always think logically. Perhaps, there's a disconnect between their emotions and reality.

Marly: Cognitive dissonance?

Dr. Kingsley: I'd say so. But probably even more than that. Likely, there's a bit of narcissism or psychotic tendencies.

Marly: Yikes. Well, maybe it's best that they haven't come forward. I'm not too keen on dealing with a psychotic.

Chapter Thirty-five

"Hello?"

"Hey, there," Dee said. "Just checking in."

"Wow, I was just about to call you. Oh, boy, do I have some news for you," Marly replied, excitedly.

"Yeah? Good, I hope."

"You'll never guess who showed up at our house the other day."

"Who?"

"My old boss!"

"No way."

"Yes, and it was wild."

"What happened?"

"You know I'd always been suspicious of the guy who was tailing me through the park the day I was hit, right? So, I—we—reported it, Craig and I did to the police. In my heart, I really thought it was my boss. I could have sworn the driver looked just like him."

"Yeah, I remember. You mentioned that at the hospital . . . unbelievable."

"Can you imagine? So, I couldn't tell if it was a Jag he was driving or not, as the car was just too close to my bumper. And then it started to downpour. So, anyway, I really didn't know until *boom*, he hit my car. Or *someone* hit my car. But hold on. Here's the thing. Turns out, it *was* my boss who was tailing me!"

"That jerk!"

"No, no. wait. Hold on. Listen, yes, it *was* him. He was tailing me. But he's not the one who hit me."

"How do you know?"

"He came to our house to tell us that he hadn't been the one. He explained everything."

"So, if he's not guilty of the hit-and-run, who is?"

"That's the riddle of the day."

"Oh, boy. Well, do you believe him?"

"Actually, I have no reason not to. I mean, really, it's a shame because, for one, he says there's no front-end damage to his car. And for two, his story pans out."

"What's his story?"

"He was en route to Christine."

"Christine?"

"The lady—my former co-worker, Christine Kirsh."

"Oh, yeah, the lady from MNN. The one who . . . "

"Yep. I guess he was hoping to talk her down from the ledge or wherever she was standing in the park."

"Too sad."

"I know. So, that was his excuse for high-tailing it through the park, which is totally plausible."

"So, now the guilty driver is still on the loose?"

"Sounds like you're describing a deranged killer."

"I am. The driver *did* almost kill you, Marly."

"True, I did come pretty close. But there was a hero to my rescue. If not for Ethan, I'd probably have drowned. You must be so proud of him, Dee."

Dee sighed. "Yeah, he's a hero, but our hero, unfortunately, has pneumonia."

"Oh, no, that's awful."

"He's in the hospital."

Marly's heart sank. If he hadn't come to her rescue in the cold waters of the river, he'd probably be fine right now. Guilt swept over her. She didn't want to say it out loud, but she knew he was sick probably because of her.

"What hospital?"

"Sacred Heart."

Chapter Thirty-six

MARLY AWOKE THE FOLLOWING morning feeling a strong urge to go to the hospital to see Ethan. Her heart broke for his condition. The cancer may have possibly been part of why his immune system couldn't handle the cold water. She wasn't a doctor, but it made sense to her. It also made sense that if not for her car accident, this wouldn't have happened to him. She only blamed herself for his situation, and the guilt laid heavy. Even though he told her everything was okay, perhaps it was just to save face.

Marly entered the hospital and walked through the lobby to the information desk. After receiving a photo ID badge and Ethan's room number, she got into one of the waiting elevators and pushed the button for the fourth floor. A nervous twinge gripped her gut. She didn't know what to expect. *Could he talk? Would he be receptive to seeing her while he was bedridden?* The questions circled in her mind.

Rounding the corners of the long, sterile hallways, she spotted the sign for directions to his room. She made a right and headed down the quiet corridor to #4007. At the approach to his room, she heard male voices talking inside. Taking a peek while standing outside the door, she saw a couple of men at the foot of his bed. The spirit of the room lent to lighthearted male bonding and laughter. Marly paused, wondering if she should go in or wait until the visitors left? Thinking it would be best to wait, she went back down the hall and entered the ladies' room to kill some time. Later, when she came out and headed for his room again, things sounded quiet as she neared the door. She paused for a moment and then stepped inside.

At first, Ethan appeared to be asleep. As she approached the bed, his eyes fluttered open. A quick smile spread across his face.

"Hey, Ethan."

"Hey, Sunshine."

"Hope this isn't a bad time to visit."

"How could it be a bad time?"

"I guess it's now my turn to visit you."

"Where are my flowers?"

"I told them to deliver a bouquet this morning. Guess they're late. Can't depend on anyone these days."

His lips curled up. "Liar."

"So, how are you feeling? Dee mentioned that you have pneumonia."

He shrugged. "We didn't know whether it was COVID or pneumonia. It was hard to tell. The hospital was the best place to get checked out for certain. Doctor's orders."

"You don't look bad for being laid up in bed," she encouraged.

"Thankfully, I don't have COVID. That's what the doctor said. Had a fever earlier, but it's gone now."

"Do you have an appetite?"

"They brought me chicken soup. That's about all I can get down."

"You're not nauseous, are you?"

"No. Just tired."

"I should go."

"No. Stay."

A quiet hush fell over the room. She sensed something different in him. *Was he ill with anything serious besides pneumonia? Was this part of the cancer scare that Dee had frantically spoken of not too long ago?* She didn't want to bring up the "c" word, but the tension in the room was palpable.

Marly took a seat by the window and glanced out at the view. Turning back to him, his eyes met with hers. Something was on his mind. She felt self-conscious but in a good way, and at one point they both started talking over each other at the same time.

"Oops, sorry," she said with a giggle. "Go ahead."

"No, no. Go ahead," he insisted.

"Okay, but listen . . . seriously, I just hope you get better soon." She paused. "I hate seeing you in this condition."

"I'll be okay."

Will you? I hope so. She had reservations about verbalizing aloud what was on her mind, but throwing caution away, she forged ahead.

"Um, sorry to bring this up, but remember when you told me you were okay . . . that is, with regard to cancer?" Her words came out hesitantly. "I assumed you meant that you really didn't have cancer. Is that true? Did the doctor get the diagnosis wrong?"

Ethan's eyes met hers again. "Listen, about the cancer . . . " He shook his head. "I don't have it."

"Oh, that's wonderful to hear!"

"I'm not sure how to say this, but I . . . um, I never had cancer."

"But the letter from the doctor that Dee found. What was that?"

"About that. Well, she found it in the trash can, but I never meant for her to see it."

"You were hiding it from her?"

"Yeah." He blew out a breath. "Because it was fake."

"Fake?"

He nodded.

"Your letter or the diagnosis?"

"Both."

"I don't understand."

"See, I wrote the letter and then tossed it."

"But why would you have written it in the first place?"

"It was a stupid idea, I know." He stopped talking and just looked at her. In the silence, he made a face, appearing embarrassed. His cheeks flushed and he shook his head. "Truth is, I wanted Dee to . . . I don't know how to say it, but I kind of wanted to get out . . . move on . . . I care and all, but I hoped she'd just lose faith that I'd ever want to marry her—or even could."

"Move on . . . from her?"

He nodded.

Marly was stunned by his revelation. "Wow, I don't know what to say."

"Well, before you say anything, please understand that it was a cowardly thing to do, and that's why I caught myself and just decided to chuck the idea altogether."

"You're not a coward, Ethan."

"But I'm not proud of myself for even considering it."

"Yeah, but you had second thoughts and decided to get rid of it."

"True, but it backfired on me. She *found* it."

"And she really thinks you have cancer."

Ethan hung his head. "I know. And nothing I say can alleviate her concern. I can't tell her it's a fake letter, and the more I tell her that it was a misdiagnosis, the more she second guesses me."

"You're in deep sneakers, I hate to tell you."

In the silence between them, Marly felt the weight of his stare, like a magnetic beam penetrating through her.

"Marly, for the past year or more, my feelings for Dee have shifted. I don't know how or why, but I've become . . . how do I say it? I guess I've just been distracted."

"Distracted?"

"To say the least."

"How so?"

"By someone else."

"I see. Well, these things happen, I guess. You're only human."

"Someone who occupies my thoughts day and night." He slapped his arm down on the bed sheet. "Only problem is that I can't really have her. Not the way I'd like to, anyway."

"Why can't you have her the way you'd like?"

"She's married."

"Ah, must be pretty frustrating for you."

"Her image is always there."

"Sounds like you've got it bad."

"I can't shake her no matter how hard I try."

"Does she know that you have feelings for her?"

Ethan stifled a smile. "She does now."

Chapter Thirty-seven

Blood rushed to Marly's face. Embarrassed, shocked, and surprised all at once, she froze. Ethan looked at her with such emotion in his eyes, the strong gaze practically knocked her over. She didn't know what to say and stumbled her way self-consciously into the first words that popped into her head.

"You're not meaning what . . . what I think you're meaning, are you, Ethan?"

"What do you think?" He smiled. "Yes."

"I . . . I don't know what to say."

"You don't have to say anything. It must be my meds making me spill this all to you." He covered his face with one hand. "I'm sorry. This is so embarrassing."

Not to me, Ethan. I've had a few thoughts about you, too, over the years.

She glanced up at him self-consciously and then shifted her gaze back down. Meeting his eyes suddenly felt awkward. She always knew they had a special kind of connection. It began years ago. With some people there's an immediate attraction, and she'd felt that with Ethan. Of course, with both of them being spoken for, she never thought anything would come of it. They just met at the wrong time in their lives.

"I don't want to make you uncomfortable or anything, but we clicked from day one. And you know if there was ever anything I could do for you, I would."

Oh, Ethan.

Marly melted at his words. She didn't want to go as far as to agree with him about her own feelings—at least not out loud. But truth be told, she adored him. Being married to Craig was her life, and she'd be a shell of a woman without him, but she had entertained her own warm thoughts about Ethan many times. More than she could count. She often felt butterflies in her stomach at seeing him. *Yes, we do click, Ethan. You got that right.*

"If I weren't married, would things look different between us?"

He nodded. "Yes, it would."

Marly felt a rush inside at his words. The honesty bowled her over, and it endeared him to her all the more. His full disclosure was probably the meds doing the talking, like he'd said, because normally he was a very private person and kept things close to the vest. The heady feeling of knowing Ethan had such feelings felt overwhelming and gave her pause. It was good to know her flower's bloom hadn't fallen off in his eyes. *What would life look like with Ethan? Could it ever be?* Marly let her mind drift for a moment but quickly pulled herself back to the present.

"But what about Dee?"

"What about her?"

"Your relationship. It's been so long that you've been together. Most people would have been married by now."

"Marly, I'm not the marrying kind of guy."

Marly understood. He'd mentioned it before. It wasn't a secret. The only problem was that keeping Dee as just a girlfriend after all these years seemed odd. When her friends ask about when she'll be getting married, what can she tell them? It's probably embarrassing for her by now. But that was their business. Marly couldn't interfere.

Everything had changed now, and she wasn't sure what to do with the information, nor what to do with her own feelings besides bury them. Even worse, how will Dee feel when she finds out? Marly couldn't let that happen. No, Ethan must never tell

Dee the reason for his distance and detachment. It was a sad situation all the way around.

"Well, I think I better let you get some sleep."

"You don't have to go."

"Yes, I do. The only cure for you is to rest."

"Thanks, doc. Is that your professional opinion?"

Marly rolled her eyes. "Take it for what it's worth." She moved toward the door.

"It was good to see you, kiddo. Thanks for stopping by."

She turned and smiled. "My pleasure, Ethan."

Chapter Thirty-eight

MARLY STEPPED OUT OF Ethan's room feeling lighter than when she first walked in. It was as though her feet didn't touch the ground on her way to the elevator. *High* was the word. Yes, she felt high. His words came unexpectedly and yet, in a way, she always knew how he felt. Though things had always remained above board and there was no guilt or shame. Still, Marly felt in a way that she betrayed her best friend.

As she stepped out of the hospital, the brisk early evening air felt good on her face, cooling off the heat of the moment earlier in Ethan's room. She pulled out the key fob provided by the insurance company for the loaner Hyundai and was about to click open the door lock when something caught her eye. A particular vehicle drew her attention. A black SUV. The front of the grill and bumper had a large indentation as though something had crushed it. *Oh, my god.* Her heart jolted. Without hesitation, she turned back toward the hospital and headed straight to the Security office adjacent to the main entrance.

"Excuse me," Marly began when she approached a burly man seated at the desk engaged in a crossword puzzle. "Can you help me with something?"

"Sure." He put down his pencil. "What do you need?"

"I need to report something that's in the parking lot."

The security guard raised an eyebrow. "What is it?"

"A car—an SUV. There's a dent in it."

"Did you hit the car?"

"No, no, nothing like that." Marly shook her head. "In fact, quite the opposite."

"How so?"

"I was in an accident early last week. A hit-and-run. And I think it may be the suspect's car, the one the police are looking for regarding in my accident."

The security guard bore a puzzled look. "Excuse me, but you sound familiar. I'm trying to place you. Do you—"

"Yes," she said before he finished. "I'm Marly Maines."

He snapped his fingers and smiled. "Yeah, the news. That's where I know you from."

She lent a mock grin. People always reacted the same way to her when they recognized her name. *I didn't cure cancer or anything like that* is what she longed to say to them whenever they lit up. "Yeah, so about my accident—"

"I heard about that. Happened right over here, right?" He pointed out the window.

"Yes, in Valley Forge Park."

"And didn't something else happened that night, too? Didn't a woman drown or something? I heard it was all kind of crazy over there."

"Well, I almost drowned. My car ended up in the creek. Though another person *did* drown. She fell from a precipice overlooking the creek."

"Oh, yeah. Wow." He frowned. "Shame."

"I know. Crazy night. So, yeah, about the car. Can you call the police for me? I think they'd be very interested in seeing this vehicle. It's parked in Row E about midway down from the main driveway."

"Sure thing, Ms. Maines. I'll call them right away."

Chapter Thirty-nine

MARLY LEFT THE SECURITY office and walked back to the parking lot. Vague pieces of memory flashed back as she recalled the accident. In the pouring rain, she barely made out the type or color of the car tailing close behind her but thought it might be either silver or gray. John Strauss's car was a silver Jag, but there was no front-end damage to his car he'd told her and the police. Claiming he turned off the main road for a secondary road that led over the creek, reckoned him not guilty. His car was not involved in hitting hers, although he was on the road at the same time. It probably would have taken a heavier car to knock her over the embankment. An SUV easily could have done that.

Clicking on the key fob, the lights to the Hyundai flashed in the near distance. Before she got to the car, something in her peripheral vision drew her attention. In the bright fluorescence of the light pole, she paused at seeing a figure.

"Hello, Marly," came the female voice.

"Jen?"

"Yes, how are you, Marly?"

"I'm good."

"I'm sure you are. Better after seeing Ethan, right?"

Marly flinched. "Ethan? What do you mean?"

"Like you think I don't know?"

"Know what?"

Jen gave a fake laugh. "C'mon, Marly, everyone knows."

Marly's nerves tightened. "What are you talking about, Jen?"

Jen's face morphed into something Marly didn't recognize as though the woman put on a demon mask. It gave her a creepy feeling. She knew the red-headed woman had a wild side and was known to be high strung, but Marly wasn't prepared for what was happening.

"I heard you talking to Ethan a little while ago in his room."

Marly's ears grew warm. "Where were you?"

"Just outside the door."

"Why didn't you come in?"

"I didn't want to interrupt the *hot* conversation."

"It wasn't *hot,* Jen. I don't even know what you're referring to."

"Uh huh." Jen smirked. "I've seen the way Ethan looks at you. Tonight wasn't the first time, no. That look in his eyes . . . anyone can see what he's thinking when he looks at you. You'd have to be blind not to."

"Jen, I think you're way out of bounds here."

"Am I? I know way more than you think I do."

"You know . . . just what?" Marly grew more unnerved by the minute.

"Let's just say a little birdy told me. And Dee has seen the way he looks at you, too. And it bothers her."

"Dee has never said anything to me about Ethan like what you're inferring. How dare you!"

"Never mind that. And by the way, I want to tell you something else. You're barking up the wrong tree with that investigative story you're writing."

"How do you know about that?"

"Believe me, I have my ways. Trust me, I know."

"What in the world are you *on,* Jen? You're not making any sense."

"Oh, really?"

"Yeah, really. What's my story to you? How's it your business?"

"I just want to let you know that your story is fake news."

"Fake, how's that?"

"It's fake because you don't have the right facts. The details are all wrong."

"How do you know anything about the details? Are you talking about the Libby Kirshka Halloween night story?"

"Of course. What other story is there? You were working on it when you were fired."

"I wasn't fired. I was let go in a cost-cutting effort. It's called a layoff. Happens to the best of employees."

"Spin it any way you want to, but you're out of a job and out of an assignment, yet you continue to think that you can get the story published. Well, I have news for you. Your details about *who dunnit* are totally false."

"How do you know?"

"How do I know?" She faked another laugh. "I know because I was with her that night."

"With Christine?"

"Yeah, with her and the kid, Stevie, she used to babysit when he was little."

"So, why are you telling me all this?"

"My friend, Chrissy, is dead because of you."

"Me? You're wacked, Jen. Seriously? How can you say that?"

"She's dead because she couldn't handle the stress, the guilt, and everything else when she heard the story would be coming out again. She'd buried all of her feelings and all of the remorse, but you couldn't let it die, could you? You had to stir it up again."

"I'm writing the story to serve justice to a little six-year-old girl who never got it!"

"Oh, poor Libby. Spoiled little snot-nosed princess."

"She's a human being, Jen. So, what's this to you? You saying I shouldn't report the facts of a cold case because someone's feelings could get hurt?"

"Not anymore, she's dead."

"I know that, Jen. We all know that. You're saying the story shouldn't be told? I mean, what are you telling me here? You believe Christine and Steve are innocent?"

"Yes, they are. They both are."

"Okay, fine. No one is incriminating them. They were just witnesses to the last time the child was alive is all. But something happened that night, and someone has to know what it was, right?"

"It was neither of them. They didn't know anything."

"How do you know so well?"

"Because I'm the one who pushed Libby into the water."

Chapter Forty

MARLY'S SENSES REELED. HER heart pounded. She didn't know how to get out of this situation, but something had to be done. Her instincts said to run though her feet felt like clay, like in a dream with nowhere to run. When the woman reached into her purse, Marly gasped when a gun emerged.

"My friend always hated the way that girl was treated compared to herself. The way her mother doted on the little brat . . . it was disgusting." Jen sneered. "Chrissy felt like a second-class citizen all her life."

"I-I'm so sorry about what happened to Christine as a girl, I really am." Marly kept her eyes focused on the gun. "But let's reason here. There's nothing I can do for her now."

"My friend is dead because of you!" Jen barked. "And my cousin's boyfriend—the one she wants to marry—is in love with you."

"In love with me? Where'd you get that idea?"

"C'mon, Marly, don't play dumb with me. You know damn well his feelings. You can't see it? How come others know and not you? In denial much?"

"I-I don't know what you want from me."

So, you know what I want? I want you dead."

Jen raised the gun. Holding it with both hands, she fired a shot. Marly felt the whizz of the bullet, but Jen's aim was off. Miraculously, it just missed her ear. Marly lunged and seized Jen by the wrist to

126

attempt from getting shot again, making sure the gun remained facing upward. She squeezed Jen's wrist as hard as she could until the gun dropped to the ground. Marly quickly grabbed it.

Marly screamed for help. The sound of her shrill cry pierced the otherwise silent air. There were no other cars coming or going in the visitor's section of the parking area, and she feared they were alone. Marly held the gun close to her chest. Though she had no experience ever firing a gun, nor even touching one before, holding it lent a strange sort of peace. Jen could no longer hurt her, at least not with a gun.

Moments later, Marly's tension eased when the security guard she'd spoken to earlier came running across the parking lot, along with two other uniformed officers. *Just in time, thank God.*

"What's going on Ms. Maines? Put down the gun."

"I'd be happy to, sir. It's not mine, anyway." She handed it to him while glancing at Jen. "It belongs to her." Marly's body trembled as adrenaline surged through her veins. "She just tried to kill me."

Chapter Forty-one

MARLY STOOD SHIVERING IN the parking lot while giving her statement to the police officers. They questioned her and Jen, privately, each giving their side of the situation, though Marly could barely talk from nerves; her words sounded shaky and slurred. Marly wondered if they bought her story or Jen's? After all, it wasn't Jen holding the gun when the police officers and the security guard arrived. It didn't look good in Marly's opinion.

The night started off so well inside the hospital while talking to Ethan, but now things had gone south. If Marly could be anywhere else right now, it would be back in Ethan's room. If only she hadn't left at the time she did. She believed God ordained her steps; so, is this what God wanted? All this drama? Even so, she trusted him to work out the plan he had for her in this situation. *Lord, please help me.*

After speaking with the officers and describing the situation and facts of the story about being the victim here, Marly gestured to one of the cops. She pointed toward the adjacent row of cars and waved him on.

"Officer, I need to show you something." The taller officer followed as she went to the damaged SUV, not far from where they stood. "Officer, this is the car I believe hit mine"—she pointed to the dented front grill and bumper—"in the accident that happened a week ago, last Monday night at Valley Forge Park. I can't prove it, but I've got a gut feeling."

"I recall the situation, Ms. Maines"—he nodded with assurance—"and we have the case on record. Security Officer Brown was just showing us this vehicle. I was about to check for fingerprints when we heard the gun shot and your screams."

Thank God they were close by.

"Glad you're on top of it. There's been a crime here, and all I want is justice."

"The case has not gone unfinished, I can tell you that much," the tall officer explained.

"Well, it would be a step in the right direction to find out who the car belongs to."

As Marly and the tall cop walked back to the others, the second police officer stood talking to Jen. Marly hoped the investigation would give rise to the truth and Jen wouldn't try to bluff her way out of the situation. Though as Marly got closer, what she heard coming out of Jen's mouth was nonsensical. The words: *"tried to punch me"* . . . *"was threatening"* . . . *"cursed me out"* made Marly's ears burn.

"No, Jen, wrong! I never threatened you. No, not even for a minute. You're a liar!" She turned to the tall policeman. "Officer, that woman is sick. Like I told you, *she* approached *me* out of the blue as I was coming out of the hospital after visiting a friend. Now, she's turning it around. She's wacko and . . . well, I'm not going to go into it all here, but suffice it to say, she's lying."

"Ma'am, is it true that this is your gun?" the policeman inquired of Jen.

Jen nodded.

"Is it registered?"

She looked at him blankly. "I-I think so."

"I'll need to see your license and registration."

"I don't have my gun registration with me."

"I'm talking about your *vehicle* registration and license."

"I'm pretty sure the information is inside the glove box."

"Where are you parked?"

"Right over there."

"Where?"

Jen pointed in the direction of where Marly and the tall officer had been standing earlier in the adjacent row.

"Show me." He gestured with his thumb.

Everyone followed her as she made her way across the lot to her vehicle. She stopped at the damaged SUV.

He pointed to the dented grill. "Is this your vehicle?"

"Uh huh."

Marly's jaw dropped. "That's *your* SUV, Jen?"

"Please show me your license and registration, ma'am," he repeated.

Jen pulled out a key and unlocked the door.

"Oh, my God, you're the one who ran me off the road!"

Jen gave Marly a dirty look as she hopped inside and rifled through the glove compartment. She came back out of the vehicle and handed the information to the officer. "I never said I was the one driving. Maybe I was, maybe I wasn't."

"Either way, you must have known and you didn't come forward."

"Ms. Morrison," the officer said while reading the name on her license. "We're familiar with the hit-and-run situation in Valley Forge Park last week. If what you're saying is true, that's a felony. Whether you were involved or not, I think you need to get an attorney."

Chapter Forty-two

Session:

Dr. Kingsley: So, how are you're doing?

Marly: Actually, I've been better.

Dr. Kingsley: I'm sorry. A lot of drama these days?

Marly: You could say that.

Dr. Kingsley: I'm all ears.

Marly: You remember about my accident?

Dr. Kingsley: Yes, the hit-and-run. Awful. I saw the write-up in the paper, too.

Marly: It was brutal.

Dr. Kingsley: Indeed. I'm so sorry that happened to you, Marly.

Marly: The accident was no accident. It was but . . . well. Anyway, you know that Jen is a suspect, right?

Dr. Kingsley: Goodness, no! I'm shocked to hear that. She was the driver of the car that ran you off the road?

Marly: I'm sure she was. Don't know if she will ever admit it or not, but my gut says it was her. Her SUV had front end damage.

But there's always the question of whether she acted alone or with someone else.

Dr. Kingsley: Who else were you thinking?

Marly: I'm just wondering if her cousin Dee could have been with her. You know, maybe it was her jealousy or something. I don't know. I'm just thinking that maybe Jen put a bug in Dee's ear about her boyfriend's feelings . . . his feelings for . . .

Dr. Kingsley: You?

Marly: Yes.

Dr. Kingsley: Anything's possible.

Marly: Jen did confess that it wasn't her idea to do it, but who knows if she's telling it straight.

Dr. Kingsley: Idea? What do you mean?

Marly: The idea to run me off the road.

Dr. Kingsley: I can't even imagine.

Marly: Apparently, my former co-worker, Christine, needed help in squelching a story—my story about the cold case I was pursuing. She and Jen had been close friends since they were teenagers. So, I guess Jen volunteered to help Christine, and together they devised the plot to get rid of the story. And Jen was the one to carry it out. Only I got caught in the collateral damage. That's my take on it, anyway.

Dr. Kingsley: Such a shame. So, why did she want the story squelched so badly?

Marly: A couple of reasons. One, because it would drag her boyfriend's name through the mud again, and neither she nor her boyfriend, who was also her boss, wanted to go through that kind of bad publicity. Her boss is John Strauss . . . or *was* her boss. He's the Vice President of MNN. He's got a lot riding on his reputation.

Dr. Kingsley: That's plausible.

Marly: And two . . . well, it's not a pretty picture at all, but I guess her guilt got to her. She felt guilty for her sister's death. She'd always been jealous of the attention her sister got from everyone. Frankly, I think she must have been a little *touched*.

Dr. Kingsley: The little girl?

Marly: No. I think Christine became mental after a while. And, sorry to say, Jen is definitely an odd duck in my humble opinion.

Dr. Kingsley: Shame. Still seems odd to me. All that drama for a story.

Marly: Yeah, but keep in mind Jen knew about Ethan, and when she found out he had a soft spot for me, well . . . that was all the arsenal she needed to carry out her little stunt. She wanted to defend her cousin's interests and also help out her old friend at the same time. Or she wanted him for herself.

Dr. Kingsley: Perhaps all three. Jealousy isn't called the green-eyed monster for nothing. So sad.

Marly: Do you think she's psychotic? Jen, that is?

Dr. Kingsley: I'm not at liberty to divulge, but I can't say that she doesn't have some baggage.

Marly: How long have you known about her . . . well, condition?

Dr. Kingsley: A while. That's one of the reasons I decided to employ her as my secretary. That way, I could give her some help while keeping an eye on her. It's no wonder she recently asked for some personal time off. Now, the picture is coming together.

Marly: One odd thing is that Jen brought up my personal life— something I shared with you in confidence—about Ethan. And she took it all wrong, too. She twisted everything into a big lie.

Dr. Kingsley: Well, our doctor-patient confidentiality precludes me from revealing anything pertinent to your private information. I'm not sure how Jen knew of anything, but rest assured, she won't be working here any longer and will no longer be a threat to your privacy.

Chapter Forty-three

THREE MONTHS LATER . . .

The room thrummed with low-key murmuring, typical of a large gathering of dinner guests at a grand annual news media event. White tablecloths, ornately flowered centerpieces, crystal glasses, and silverware all sparkled in the glow of golden candelabra lighting.

As she walked into the room, Marly felt a sudden wave of self-consciousness. Never one to be squeamish with on-air speaking, this felt different. She didn't quite have her bearings even with Craig by her side. The fact that she'd been invited to the event surprised her when the invitation arrived by mail last month. Even though she was no longer employed by MNN, apparently, it didn't have any bearing on her being welcome. She assuaged herself silently. *You belong here, Marly.* Her nine-year history in the news business brought her to this moment, not the fact that she hadn't received a paycheck in several months.

"Where do we sit?" Craig asked. "There must be a hundred tables in here."

Marly scanned the room. "Not that many." She checked the card printed with their names and table number. "Says we're number twenty-one." She pointed toward the middle where several people were already seated. "It's over there."

Marly and Craig weaved through the maze of tables.

"Hi," Marly greeted with a smile to the other table mates. Niceties were exchanged with the folks from competing news agencies and publications, along with their spouses. Marly's nerves finally settled when she realized they were just ordinary people seated for yet another ordinary public event. No big deal. After a while, a tall, white-haired man walked up onto the stage and addressed the room.

"Good evening, everyone," he said into the microphone.

Marly recognized him from MNN—Richard Marx—the guy who ran the show behind the scenes and the man who ranked directly above her former boss, John Strauss. She didn't know Richard well, but in her brief interactions with him every so often in the hallway, he seemed like a decent guy.

"That's Mr. Marx," she whispered to Craig. "He's a VIP but very down-to-earth."

"I want to thank *Newsmedia* for the privilege to host the 38th annual Keystone Media Awards Banquet," he continued. "Thank you for your support and thanks to everyone for being here."

He made some small talk and shared the itinerary for the evening before the servers came and delivered lobster with crabmeat, asparagus in hollandaise sauce, Caesar salad, and relish trays. The wait staff hovered around the tables as though in a choreographed dance while serving and, later, bussing. Afterward, they brought wheeled carts bearing decadent looking desserts on a carousel.

After dinner, Richard talked a bit about the early pioneer days of radio and TV news gathering and, later, a short film lent to the founding of some of the larger news networks.

Marly glanced at Craig. He came to support her, but the expression on his face told her the night was dragging. *Poor Craig.* Of course, not knowing anyone and not being much of a people-person, he would have been more entertained by reading a book while waiting in the lobby than having to hang through an awards banquet. She couldn't blame him. Though she smiled, inwardly, at his effort to at least try to be present for her.

"Thanks for coming, hon," she whispered in his ear. "Appreciate the effort."

He nodded while chugging back his drink.

"Listen, we don't have to stay much longer."

"I'm okay. Do your thing. I know you've gotta do some schmoozing in this business."

"Ugh," she replied. "Hate schmoozing."

"I know. Just razzing you."

While the evening wore on, she checked the time. As it neared nine-thirty, she couldn't stop yawning. Another quick glance at Craig, and his eyes appeared to be glazed over.

"You wanna go now?" she asked, leaning closer.

"I'm ready, but it's up to you, hon. Whatever you want to do."

She signaled with a nod that she was ready and was about to stand when Richard stepped back on stage.

"There's something special on the agenda for this evening that we haven't done in the past. While all of our journalists are singular and their work altogether above par, we'd like to call attention to a particular one tonight. We'd like to honor someone for an inspiring determination to bring a long, almost forgotten story to light. It's been a cold case in Philadelphia for nearly a decade. It took a spirit of dogged conviction, determination, and a whole lot of courage and heart. So, tonight, we'd like to honor the journalist who endured so much to bring the Libby Kirshka story to the public consciousness. For her bravery in seeking justice for the child, we'd like to award Marly Maines with the Keystone Medallion for journalistic integrity."

The room erupted in a thunderous applause. Struck by the serendipity, Marly froze for a second. Glancing at Craig clapping along with the others brought tears to her eyes. All of the work she'd accomplished to get the story to print, despite being laid off and almost losing her life, had been worth it in that moment.

Marly stood and approached the stage, and Richard handed her the award while wrapping an arm around her waist. Smiling, she stepped up to the microphone.

"Oh, wow. This is so unexpected . . . I'm honored and grateful . . . thank you all so much."

Never one to care much for overt praise, she kept her remarks short and sweet. On her way back to the table while the audience applauded, she heard a familiar voice call her name. She turned to see a hand waving from one of the back tables. *Dee?* Next to Dee was Jason Samuels from MNN's marketing group. *Jason?* Marly checked out the whole table and nowhere in the group of people did she notice Ethan. *Hmmm . . . Dee was on a date with another guy? Had she and Ethan finally broken up? Sure looked like it.* Marly waved back.

In that moment, Ethan's image came to mind. Tall, handsome Ethan. She wondered how he was doing and remembered the connection they shared—and probably always would. With all the distractions around her at that moment, there was no time to dwell on her feelings, but her heart tugged for him, and she wished he could have been there. He would have been happy for her.

Marly was grateful for the information on the hit-and-run that came out recently, stating the incident did not include Dee at all. Jen had acted alone in her nefarious venture on the roadway in the park, and Dee had been as shocked as anyone to hear the details of what happened. It looked like Marly's friendship with Dee overcame more than one hurdle—and survived. Sadly, Jen's future hurdles were just beginning.

Back at the table, Craig looked tired yet happy for her. His eyes danced as he stood and put his arms around her.

"Did you know about this?" she asked him.

"Nope."

"Sure?"

"Positive, honey. I really didn't know."

Marly felt a tap on her shoulder. She turned to see her old boss, John Strauss. His face held a wide grin.

"Congratulations, Marly."

"Thanks, John."

"I'm proud of you. The story couldn't have been written better if I'd done it myself."

"Aww, thank you. Means a lot."

"By the way, there's something I've been meaning to ask you."

"What?"

"I'd like to know if you'd consider coming back to MNN?"

Marly's heart soared. "Um, well, yeah, of course. In what capacity?"

"How about your old job back?"

She smiled. "Sounds good to me."

"I'm glad." He paused. "But . . . you know what. I'm not sure if that's the right position for you. I think you may have grown out of that job. How about I put you in charge of the department . . . say, News Bureau Chief? How does that sound?"

"John, I don't know what to say?"

"How about *yes*?"

Marly shook her head in disbelief wondering if this were just a dream. She liked the way it was playing out. Having only nightmares, lately, this moment refreshed her in more ways than one. She felt the Spirit of God with her and a door that had been closed now slowly opened in her mind's eye. Behind it, glowed a golden light. She extended her hand to him.

"Yes, I'd love to."

The End